Reign of the Buffalo

Reign of the Buffalo

Book 2

Nathan Jay

JNJ Publishing LLC

CONTENTS

1

Little Brother

When Michael opened his eyes, all he could see were the bright stars in the night sky. The cool air rushed into his nostrils, and he breathed deeply. Michael thought he was on the porch of his Great Grandfather's house with his brother Wilson and his parents. But after a few seconds, he knew he wasn't there. Michael began to panic. Where was he? Where was his family? Something made him feel strange – like dozens of eyes were watching him. Michael attempted to look around but found that his head and neck were locked inside a wooden vice-like contraption. He tried to stand, but his body was strapped to a wooden board.

"Wilson?" Michael asked as his panic grew. He tried moving his head once more. After failing to free himself, Michael tried to lift his arms and legs. He was unsuccessful.

Suddenly the nightmare he had returned to him like a tidal wave. The worms that ate through his chest; the excruciating pain he felt as the long snakelike creatures pulled him by his ribcage across the yard; the strange man that was waiting for him at the edge of the forest.

Michael's heart was pounding now. He had no idea of where he was or what was going on.

"Mom! Dad!"

Those were the words that Michael attempted to speak.

Instead, what came out of his mouth was,

"Father, please save me!"

The words he spoke startled him, not for what he said, but because of how different his voice sounded. Michael didn't recognize the mono-tone pleas of desperation coming from his throat. They weren't his. The words belonged to a person he didn't know—a stranger. The words were both desperate and terrifying at once, like a lost soul crying out for help in a cold dark room that no one would hear.

Michael tried again to cry out for his mother and father.

"Dad! Mom!"

But, once again, the deep voice pushed forth words that belonged to someone else.

Suddenly a pale face with a gray beard leaned over Michael.

"Goddamn, Jimmy! This boy looks scared to shit!" the man's country twanged voice exclaimed through bean-covered teeth. The mixture of bad hygiene and alcohol made Michael want to vomit. He could see the evil dancing in the man's eyes like flames in a fire.

"He has every right to be scared," said a voice to Michael's right. "I'm about to show you sons of bitches how this machine works."

"You sure this thing is for real? I mean, will we be able to see his brains come out of his ears and eyeballs? And he'll be awake when it happens? Impossible."

"Trust me, fellas. I designed my machines to inflict maximum damage while also having the subject aware of what is happening to their bodies. They feel everything and can see everything. That's what you paid your money for, ain't it?"

"You'd better not be bullshitting us. I came from Kentucky with a wagon full of these coons. Lazy, good-for-nothing bastards cost me an arm and a leg, and I need to get rid of them. If I have to carry them back, you're paying for everything. I better get my money's worth."

"Trust me. You'll get your money's worth. The pain you will see on his face is delicious. Better than sex."

Suddenly a random voice shot up from the group.

"Maybe that's because you're doing it wrong!"

The sound of laughter rose into the night air. Michael began shaking as he digested what the man had told the men. He guessed that 10 or 20 men were standing around him, all anticipating his torture and death.

"Fuck you bastards!" the child yelled. Once more, the words he heard were not his own.

"I forgive you," are the words that came from Michael's mouth.

At that moment, Michael felt drops of water falling on his face. He stared up into the sky and saw that thick clouds had appeared. Flashes of lightning moved randomly amongst the masses of water vapor. Suddenly a more brilliant thunderbolt struck, and Michael jumped. Briefly, he saw the faces of the men closest to him, and he screamed. The men were not what they seemed to be. On the surface, they were human with faces like ordinary men. But floating just beneath their skin were creatures that only the light of the storm revealed. Some of the men had red eyes that resembled snakes. Others had holes within the center of their faces that hid more sinister creatures deep within. Some men had terrifying ghosts shrieking inside them, and others had demons screaming out to Michael directly, threatening to disembowel him and eat his soul.

Michael closed his eyes and tried to think of something else. He wanted to scream, but only whispers came out of his mouth.

"I'm going to die," he whispered in that strange voice.

Michael finally understood why the men were there. He understood who he was and what was happening. Michael was in a reenactment of some kind. But instead of being in his own body, he was a slave, perhaps the first to be taken to hell in one of Mr. Green's torture machines. It was a ritual in which the evil Mr. Green sent souls to hell, and the monsters surrounding them were witnesses of the deed.

As he lay squirming within the wooden contraption, Michael squeezed his eyes shut and tried to tell himself he was dreaming. Soon other sensations within his body came into existence. Although he couldn't see his chest, he could feel something moving inside.

"Worms," he mouthed without speaking. The thought of what the creatures were doing to his insides made him want to vomit. He could feel them slithering and biting, brushing up against other organs as they moved through his torso.

"Are you going to start this goddamned machine or what?" asked an unfamiliar voice.

"Yeah!" complained the large group of men in unison.

Michael opened his eyes. As soon as he did, a face leaned over and smiled. A giant shudder shot through the child's body. It was the man he'd seen at the edge of the forest – Mr. Green! Michael screamed as he felt a giant rush of pain in his chest. The shirt he was wearing rose, and Michael screamed even louder. The child could feel the worms stretching his skin, trying to move towards Mr. Green as he stood over the boy.

Michael closed his eyes once more and prepared for the worst. He ran his thumbs up and down the sides of his trousers, waiting nervously for the evil man to hurt him.

"Please! I'm just a kid!" Michael screamed. This time, the words from the child's mouth were in a different language. Mr. Green grabbed the handle of the machine and began to twist it.

"I don't want to die! Mommy!" Michael yelled.

One of the men moved close.

"What is he saying?" the man asked.

"He knows I'm about to take him to hell," replied Mr. Green with a sinister smile on his face.

Michael grabbed the sides of his jeans as his captor turned the machine once more. He could feel the pressure building on his head with each twist of the machine's handle. It wasn't long before his vision became blurry. Soon all the voices Michael heard around him were just white noise.

"Wilson..." Michael whispered.

Suddenly the sky above him became bloody red, and the clouds looked like balls of fire in the night sky. Michael began sweating, his breathing labored. He could feel himself losing consciousness, something pulling him down into darkness. Michael started blinking his eyes furiously, trying to stay awake. He grabbed the seams of his pants, trying to hold onto anything that would keep him from being pulled into the blackness.

Just as he felt himself slipping away, Michael's fingers rubbed against something hard in his pocket.

It was the triangle!

A sense of happiness and fear ran through Michael at once. He knew the power of the triangle would allow him to escape, but he also remembered the hole the weapon had burned into the roof of his father's car. Would he also perish within their destruction in his attempt to free himself from the evil men? What would happen to the creatures inside his body?

"Okay, now watch this, boys!" yelled Mr. Green. The man moved to the opposite side of the machine and grabbed a long wooden lever. With both hands, he lifted it high and spoke to the group of men.

"As soon as I slam this lever into place, you guys are going to see some serious fireworks. Stand back!"

The crowd took a step back from Michael and stared at Mr. Green in anticipation. Mr. Green gathered his strength and was about to pull down on the stick when Michael quickly touched the triangle's three corners with his thumb. There was a buzzing sound, and the men looked around, confused. Mr. Green spun around, trying to find the location of the sound. Finally, he looked at Michael, and his eyes widened.

"WHAT?! NOOOOOOOO...."

Michael watched as Mr. Green's face began to glow a fiery red from the inside. The man started coughing violently, and smoke billowed from his nostrils and mouth. He staggered backward and fell onto the grass, gasping for air. Suddenly his whole body burst into flame. Michael watched as Mr. Green rose from the ground and ran into the forest, leaving nothing but a trail of burning grass behind him.

The other men raised their heads to the sky and released terrifying high-pitched shrieks. Their human faces melted away to reveal their actual horrifying appearances, monsters with glowing red eyes and pale, slimy skin. Their mouths were giant, with dozens of sharp fangs jutting out with black lizard-like tongues twisting uncontrollably. The men with the holes in their faces began to shake violently as the monsters within them suddenly revealed themselves - enormous hairy black spiders that hissed as they exited their human carriers. As the spiders crawled out of the men's heads, the mens' bodies dropped to the ground, reduced to nothing but a pile of lifeless flesh while the spiders scattered into the dark forest.

Suddenly everything evil burst into flame, and the monsters fell to the ground howling and screaming in agony. Michael felt the wooden table shake as the spiders that ran into the forest exploded like small landmines, their legs unable to carry them away from the power of the triangle.

The tiny drops of rain Michael felt soon became a torrential rainstorm, dumping cold water on everything. Michael blinked and tried to see through the rain. After a few moments, he could lift his head and move his arms. Finally, he freed his hands, wiped the rain from his face, and sat up. The monsters that had surrounded him were piles of smoldering ash. The burning flesh of the monsters sizzled as the rain fell on the creatures' burning skin; a foul stench filled the air that reminded Michael of roasting pork.

"Shit!" Michael exclaimed.

The curse word brought such comfort to him that he almost started crying. His voice had returned. Michael looked down at his legs and was grateful to see that he no longer lay trapped within the slave's body. His skinny brown ankles moved loosely within the large straps, and he freed himself quickly.

"I've got to get out of here," he whispered. Suddenly he remembered what he'd done to escape. He quickly rubbed his pocket and felt the triangle once more. Next, he inspected his legs, mindful of what the weapon had done to the monsters and the roof of his father's car.

"No way!" he exclaimed. Amazingly, the only damage the triangle did was to his pants; the fire had burned some of the fabric and left his legs partially exposed to the cold night air.

As soon as he stood, Michael began coughing violently. He dropped to his knees in the mud and grabbed his chest, barely able to catch his breath.

"Shit...the...worms...."

He felt the animals pushing their way up into his throat - squirming, thrashing, biting. The pain he felt was excruciating, like someone trying to shove a large, jagged tree branch down his throat. Michael took a deep breath, his last one, and everything went black.

Minutes later, Michael opened his eyes and took in a deep blood-filled breath. Muddy rainwater flooded his mouth and nose as he lay face down in a large puddle. The relentless storm dumped even more water on him than before, and Michael raised himself to his knees.

"What the fuck...." he mumbled.

Michael rubbed his throat and let out a slight cough, his mouth feeling slimy and dirty like rotten fish and sand.

That's when he saw them.

Covering the ground all around him were hundreds of long-dead white worms. The monsters bore large purple blisters like they'd been burned with a cigarette lighter, a rotten stench rising in the air. The smell was unlike anything he'd ever smelled in his life. Michael started vomiting uncontrollably. After throwing up for a few moments, he quickly jumped to his feet.

He remembered the path Mr. Green took to escape and turned to see the flames still burning. Michael ran to the other side of the clearing and entered the forest on the opposite side, hoping to avoid the man that held him captive. He pushed through the dark forest with the wet branches slapping his face and the relentless rain making it impossible for him to see.

"Where am I?" he whispered. Michael continued pushing through the cold forest, unsure of where he was going. After a few minutes, he stopped and leaned against a tree to catch his breath.

"I...can't..." he said, almost entirely out of breath.

"Run towards the house," a voice whispered through the trees. The voice startled Michael, and he spun around in all directions, trying to find out who was speaking.

"He's coming for you."

"Who's there?" asked Michael while scanning the dark forest. "Do I know you?"

Somehow the voice didn't sound terrifying. It was comforting and familiar. Michael was sure he'd heard the voice before.

"Who's there? Do I know you?"

"Go to the house."

Suddenly a thought came into Michael's head, and his eyes widened.

"Grandma Noya, is that you?"

"Go to the house."

Although the rain was pouring, Michael could see a faint light through the trees far ahead. Slowly, he walked towards the dim light.

"Grandma Noya?"

"Run, child."

"Grandma Noya? Where should I go? How do I get out of here?"

Suddenly the rain stopped, and the faint light shining through the trees ahead of Michael slowly faded away. The sound of the water falling from the leaves also stopped, casting an eerie silence over the dark forest. Michael strained his eyes to see a glimpse of the light he'd seen ahead of him.

"Grandma Noya, are you there?"

There was nothing but silence. Michael's heart started pounding, and he walked faster in the direction of the place he'd seen the light.

"Grandma Noya? It's me, Michael. I'm lost."

The voice whispered to Michael again, but it had a sense of urgency this time.

"They're coming for you. Run!"

Suddenly a huge gust of hot air blew against Michael's back, causing him to fall onto his face. The soft voice he'd heard suddenly screamed out, causing the trees to shake all around him.

"Get up! RUNNNNN!"

Michael sprang to his feet and turned to look into the forest behind him. Two creatures with glowing green eyes were searching the wet foliage. The animals had two heads and seemed to be hybrids of two monsters; one had the face of a rotting corpse with wrinkled dead skin drooping off the skull; the other head was that of an old woman with long stringy gray hair. Both monsters bit at one another as they sat atop one human body with vomit and saliva pouring from their enormous mouths.

"Arggggh....we...smell...you...." the creatures called out over and over as they ripped through the trees with their massive claws. Michael almost screamed. He could smell the pungent odor of their vomit, their enormous mouths dripping with the thick liquid as their large round eyes combed the forest searching for him.

Michael took off sprinting through the darkness. Although he couldn't see where he was going, terror propelled him through the night, forcing him to ignore the risk of hurting himself. Briars scratched his face, and he winced as he banged his head on a tree limb. Four more steps and his arm brushed against the bark of another tree, ripping the skin off. Still, Michael ignored the pain and continued running. Terrifying screams and growls rose from the shadows behind him. The sounds seemed to give wings to Michael's feet, and he concentrated on sprinting through the forest, unsure about where he was going but determined to outrun the hell approaching from behind.

2

Rescuing Michael

"Can anybody see anything?" asked a voice from behind Wilson.

"Quiet!" Wilson whispered forcefully. He didn't know the boys well enough to say who was making all the noise, and he only wanted them to stop.

"I can't see anything. What about you, Tariq? Can you see anything?" asked a different voice from the darkness.

Wilson shook his head in frustration as the noisy boys walking behind him continued talking. There was no way he'd make it to save his little brother walking with this group of loud kids. He stopped and lowered himself onto one knee. Seconds later, the three boys walking behind Wilson did the same.

"Why are we stopping?" asked Calian, the boy closest to Wilson. "Do you see something?"

Wilson touched his eye, and a dull red light enveloped the forest, making everything translucent. Carefully he searched the woods for signs of movement. A sense of calm came over him when he didn't see anything.

"Nothing yet," Wilson replied.

The boys stood and began walking again.

"This is some dumb shit," Calian said without bothering to whisper.

"Quiet!" whispered Wilson again.

The boys ignored his warning and continued talking.

"What do you mean by dumb?" asked Tariq taking his cue to abandon the hushed conversation.

"I mean, none of this shit makes sense."

Wilson gave up his cautious posture and joined the conversation.

"It never made a lot of sense to me either," Wilson confessed.

"If this Mr. Green guy is behind all this, why is he doing it? What is he trying to gain?" asked Calian.

The last boy, Takatoka, had been trying to maintain his silence, but the other boys' conversation was too much for him to bear.

"The thing that bothers me is why our families kept this from us for so long. If they knew the gates of hell would open one day, why wouldn't they bring us together sooner?" Takatoka asked.

"It doesn't take a genius to figure out why they kept us separate," replied Tariq while chuckling.

Wilson knew the answer as well.

"We all came up different, and our parents probably wanted to keep it that way for as long as they could," he exclaimed.

"That's a nice way of putting it," mumbled Tariq.

"What are you trying to say?" asked Calian.

Tariq spoke up.

"Look at my skin. Your people and mine aren't exactly in a hurry to have a neighborhood cookout."

Calian stopped walking and frowned at Tariq.

"What are you trying to say? Our people are racists?"

"Well...Cherokees did enslave some of my people."

"Fuck you! You're a liar!"

"It's true," Wilson agreed. "None of my family talked about it, but I did read about that in school."

Calian redirected his anger towards Wilson.

"Oh, so you read some bullshit in school, and that makes it true? You share our blood. Where's your loyalty to our people?"

"Look, I'm biracial. My father is mixed Cherokee, and my mother is White. But my Great Grandfather is African, and my Great

Grandmother is Cherokee. I have no ethnicity to defend more than the other. I don't need to lie."

"The reading-fucking-rainbow right here. You're part Black, aren't you?"

"Yeah. And?"

"You're tainted. You couldn't possibly know what it means to be pure Cherokee."

Wilson could feel the anger boiling inside.

"So now I have to be pureblood?"

"You're a fucking sellout."

Startled by Calian's words, Wilson's anger boiled over, and he rushed towards Calian. Just as the two boys were about to come to blows, Tariq grabbed Wilson's arm and pulled him away.

"Calian, you sound like a fucking dummy," complained Tariq. "What is this *'our blood'* and *'loyalty to our people'* bullshit?"

"Fuck you," snarled Calian.

Tariq smiled and moved closer.

"You think these evil spirits are out here killing people based on the color of people's skin? What, are they only targeting Whites? Blacks? Everyone except Cherokee? All that shit is irrelevant when it comes to hell. They want to kill everything and everybody, regardless of skin color. The only qualifier is life, and they want to take that away. You need to unlearn that nonsense your family taught you before that shit gets us killed."

"My family is my family. Maybe you don't know what having a family means because your people aren't known for staying together. Do you even know where your dad is?"

Tariq's face grew serious, and he glared at Calian in anger.

"You sure you aren't related to Mr. Green? I'm expecting you to call me a nigger at any minute. You sound dumb as fuck. And you know what they say about the parents of stupid kids, right?"

Calian walked over to Tariq.

"Are you calling my parents stupid? Say it to my face."

Tariq made a fist and moved in close to Calian.

"You sound dumb as fuck, and your parents...."

Takatoka rushed in between the two boys before Tariq could finish the sentence and separated them.

"Stop, you guys! Does any of this stuff matter? We're in this mess together now, whether we like it or not."

This statement seemed to resonate with each of the boys, and they backed away from one another. Wilson turned away from the group and continued walking. Soon the other boys followed. After walking in silence for several minutes, Calian spoke again.

"Wilson."

"What the fuck do you want? Another fight? Leave me alone."

"Why do you think Mr. Green took your brother?"

Wilson was still bothered by Calian's earlier comment and didn't want to respond. But he had to acknowledge that he'd been asking himself the same question since they started walking through the forest. It didn't make sense that Mr. Green would target Michael.

"I don't know why he took Michael."

"Doesn't that seem personal? I mean, out of a house full of people, Mr. Green chose the smallest person?"

"Michael got infected with those worms. He was the only one. Mr. Green couldn't walk onto the property to attack us because the ground was hallowed and protected. I guess he just used Michael's infection to pull him out and force us to go after him."

"Yeah, but why? There are billions of people on this earth. If this is truly the coming of hell, why did he get so particular? Something's off about this whole thing."

Wilson suddenly found himself deep in thought. Something *didn't* make sense about the whole thing. If this were indeed an all-out assault from hell, why did Mr. Green seem to target his family? Wilson had felt the man's presence in Washington and then in Asheville. Now they were in Georgia, and Mr. Green was also here. Something wasn't right. He tried thinking back to the conversations he'd had with Grandma

Noya. Maybe he missed something. Suddenly Wilson got the sinking feeling that his family hadn't been frank about what was happening.

"My grandmother told me about our land previously belonging to him. Maybe that has something to do with it."

"Maybe, but…"

Suddenly Takatoka dove on the ground and motioned to his friends.

"Get down!" Takatoka whispered.

The other boys instantly fell and pressed their faces against the grass.

"What is it?" whispered Calian, terrified of what lay ahead in the darkness.

"Up there. Past the trees. Do you see it?" asked Takatoka as he pointed ahead.

Wilson looked in the direction the boy was pointing and froze. A tiny naked girl was in the middle of the forest – levitating high in the air. Wilson's heart dropped, and he struggled to catch his breath - it was the same Cherokee girl he'd seen in Grandma Nana's backyard! Thick purple veins covered her chest and moved out through her arms and legs like a grotesque roadmap hidden beneath her pale, lifeless skin. She had a large open wound beneath her ribcage, leaking thick purplish liquid. Her arms were short and small, but Instead of having hands, dozens of long thick glowing white worms extended from her wrists like ropes, each snakelike creature opening and closing their mouths to reveal razor-sharp teeth.

"What the fuck?" asked Calian, his voice much louder than a whisper.

As soon as he spoke, the girl's head snapped in the direction of the children, and an evil toothless smile spread across her face.

"He wants you," the girl whispered in a hoarse, terrifying voice.

She raised both her slithering arms into the air and threw them down towards the ground, releasing the creatures that were dangling on her wrist. The worms emitted horrible growls and scattered towards their intended targets through the forest.

"Oh shit! Run!" yelled Calian.

The boys scattered in different directions, hoping to confuse the creatures as they knocked over trees and trampled bushes moving towards them. Takatoka remained in place, staring at the levitating girl.

"Tee! Run!" yelled Wilson. Calian watched as the boy remained frozen, staring straight ahead.

"Dude, he's toast," exclaimed Calian as the bushes flattened in front of the boy. Takatoka reached into his jeans and pulled out a lighter. As soon as he did, the brush directly in front of him flattened.

"O'siyo," whispered Takatoka.

He lit the lighter and placed the flame on his arm. Slowly the boy's body melted away into darkness. As Takatoka disappeared, the large white wormlike creature raised from the ground and opened its mouth. It snapped its jaws and cried out in anger as it missed its target.

"Shit! Where did Takatoka go?" asked Calian. There was a rustle in the trees above the boys, and they all looked up.

"I'm up here, fellas," whispered a voice from atop the trees. The boys looked up for Takatoka but only saw the swaying of leaves.

"Where are you?" asked Calian. But Wilson wasn't worried about finding Takatoka. His eyes focused on the bushes that fell as the worms made their way to each boy. Wilson touched his eyelid, and the whole forest lit up in a red haze. Wilson saw the creatures crawling on the ground towards the group. He extended his open palm towards the nearest monster and closed it as if he were grabbing something. One worm rose in the air, thrashing, and biting, trying to break free. Wilson extended his other hand and squeezed the air. The snake's body shrank in the center and then split in half, spraying a pink malodorous mist into the air.

"Holy shit, that stinks!" exclaimed Calian. Wilson gagged at the smell but couldn't cover his nose – he'd located the other beasts trying to reach them. One by one, he grabbed each of the creatures and ripped them apart. After Wilson killed the last serpent, he looked for the others.

"Please, dude, the smell. You've got to stop. I can't take it," begged Tariq before doubling over and vomiting. Upon seeing Tariq vomiting, Calian also started throwing up, causing Wilson to fight back the vomit rising in his own throat.

Suddenly there was a loud splash.

"Dude! What the fuck!" yelled Calian. Wilson looked over and saw the boy covered in vomit. Seconds later, there was a thud beside Calian. Slowly Takatoka reappeared, wiping saliva from his mouth.

"I...didn't mean...."

"You fucking threw up on me!"

The sight of Calian covered in vomit was too much for Wilson to handle. He bent over and released his load onto the grass. Wilson searched the forest for more creatures when he finished but found none. His eyes fell on the little girl still hovering in the air in the center of the woods. The other boys lost focus and seemed more concerned with Calian's situation.

"The smell...I couldn't hold it," explained Takatoka. Tariq stood to the side, a broad smile of satisfaction on his face. Only Wilson continued watching the little girl in the center of the forest.

Calian grabbed handfuls of grass and tried to wipe off his clothes.

"I should fucking kill you! What an idiot!"

"I didn't know those things would smell so bad. It was an accident."

"Guys..." mumbled Wilson as his mouth fell open.

Tariq stood and stared at the girl also.

"Um...Takatoka. Calian...."

The little girl didn't resemble the child they had seen before. Her face had hundreds of throbbing bumps that oozed puss and made her face move as if something was inside trying to get out. Large bumps rose and fell on the girl's scalp causing her head to look swollen and deformed. Suddenly a gurgling sound came from her throat, and one of the child's eyeballs popped out, a thick black goo oozing down her face.

"Come on, guys. Let's run for it!" whispered Wilson.

"Where? She's in front of us," replied Takatoka. "You want to go back to where we came from?"

Wilson thought about it for a moment before responding.

"I can teleport."

"You can? All of us?"

"Yeah. I did it with my family."

Calian shook his head in disagreement.

"Hell no. That's a horrible idea."

"Why? When I did it, we all arrived safely."

"First of all, you don't know where we'd arrive. Any place you're familiar with has probably been overrun by now. You could sit us in the middle of hell for all you know. Second of all, I'm not willing to put my life in your hands. We don't know each other that well."

"I don't know you either, but I still killed those monsters to protect you. That didn't require your trust. And when it all boils down, what choice do we have? Today it's my brother Michael that Mr. Green has, and tomorrow it could be your family."

"Sorry, dude. I'm not doing that. We have to go through her."

"Through her? Look at her! She's not playing a game. She wants to kill us!"

"I'm not scared of that little bitch. Besides, there are four of us and one of her."

Wilson looked at the girl hovering in the air, and fear gripped him. Aside from the child's horrible appearance, there was something about the girl that truly frightened him to his core.

"We need to try to avoid her. Fighting her straight up is a mistake."

Tariq started backing away with Wilson.

"I'm with Wilson on this one," said Tariq. "She scares the fuck out of me."

"Look!" yelled Takatoka.

The girl's body started swelling, and blood began pouring from her eyes. Her body shook as she began to spin, rising higher in the air.

"He will have you! You cannot hide!" she yelled as her body grew bigger and bigger.

Suddenly the girl's body exploded, sending blood and flesh everywhere.

"Come on! Let's go!" yelled Wilson as he took off running in the opposite direction. Tariq took off running behind Wilson while the other boys stayed examining the splattered remains of the demon child that had been in front of them.

"Hey! Look!" yelled Calian.

The splattered blood on the ground began to glow.

Wilson and Tariq had almost disappeared when Takatoka finally ran behind them.

"Calian, come on!" yelled Takatoka. "Let's get out of here!"

Calian remained in place.

"There's no need to run. The monster's dead now."

"Calian, let's go!"

"You go. I'm going straight ahead."

Calian took one step forward and froze – something was stopping his feet from moving. He looked down at the ground, and a cold shiver tingled his spine. Something was out of place about the soil. Although the forest's shadows hid beneath, the forest floor felt strange. Calian bent over to take a closer look. He was trapped, unable to take a step forward or backward. Although the forest was dark, the ground seemed to be moving – like it was living. Cautiously Calian extended one of his fingers to touch the ground.

Suddenly a huge mouth full of jagged teeth emerged from the darkness of the forest floor and bit off Calian's hand.

"AAAAHHHH!" Calian screamed. He yanked his arm away, spraying blood everywhere. Finally, he was able to pull his feet free.

"HELP!" he yelled as he stumbled backward, grabbing his wrist. Soon he stopped screaming, and his mouth dropped open in fear. Calian's blood seemed to illuminate the forest floor, and he could see everything. There were no leaves or grass. Instead, Calian was standing on a thin glass coating covering the ground. What lay beneath the glass truly terrified Calian – he was standing atop a burning cavern of lava and fire with thousands of demonic creatures screaming and clawing at one another to get to him. There was a hole in the place where Calian had been standing, and four of the monsters had pushed their heads through, ripping the thin glass covering away as more demons forced their way out.

"Calian! Calian!" yelled a familiar voice through the madness. Calian felt something pulling him away from the demons and turned to look. It was Takatoka.

"What happened to your hand?" Takatoka asked as he removed his belt and tied it around Calian's forearm.

Dazed and confused, Calian could only stare at the ground, unable to explain.

"Come on! Let's get out of here!"

Finally, Calian spoke.

"There's no place to run. They're everywhere!"

"What do you mean?"

"Look at the ground! Can't you see them?"

Takatoka looked at the ground and kept pulling Calian.

"I don't see anything."

Takatoka and Calian had caught up with Wilson and Tariq by this time. The boys took one look at Calian's missing hand and started to panic.

"Shit! What the fuck happened?" asked Tariq.

"I don't know. I tried asking Calian, but he's in shock or something," replied Takatoka.

Wilson looked at Calian's arm and frowned.

"Maybe you should try teleporting Calian back," whispered Takatoka.

"I would, but I'm not sure about what would happen. Calian has an open wound, and I don't want to hurt him more. Someone's going to need to take him back to my parents."

"Nah, man," complained Tariq. "We're all going to have to go back. There's no way one person can make it back with a wounded person."

Suddenly Calian started shaking and staring at the ground.

"Can't you guys see them?" he asked. "They're everywhere! We've got to get out of here!"

Wilson tapped his eye again and looked around. He saw the splattered remains of the ghost child on the far end of the forest emitting a strange red glow, but beyond that, he saw nothing. Wilson looked at Calian and saw the same glowing liquid all over Calian's shoe and arm. He inspected the other boys looking for the same luminous fluid. Fortunately, no one else had any of the devilish liquid on them. Wilson touched his eye, and everything returned to normal.

"The girl's bodily fluids seem to be poison," said Wilson. "It's all over Calian, and it's probably making him see things."

Although the other boys could not see what Calian could see, they each took a step back from Calian, afraid that they would get some of the girl's blood on themselves.

"He's not hallucinating. Something bit his fucking hand off," said Tariq as he continued staring at Calian's missing appendage.

"Calm down, Calian. We'll get you out of here," replied Wilson.

Still, the more Calian stared at the ground, the wilder he became. He started inching away from the others, jumping wildly off the forest floor as if trying to avoid stepping on something.

"We've got to get out of here! Now!"

Calian took off running into the forest, leaving his friends behind. The boys chased him.

"Calian! Stop!" they all yelled.

But all that Calian could see was the thin glass he was running on and the thousands of monsters scrambling in the burning world underneath him, trying to break through to take him.

"We've got to get away!" he screamed back to his friends.

Wilson screamed to Calian as they tried to catch up.

"What's your power?" he asked.

Startled by the question, Calian stopped running, sat down on the ground, and closed his eyes.

"My...power...okay," he whispered.

Calian placed a finger in the center of his forehead and began whispering.

"What is he doing?" asked Tariq.

"I guess he's using his powers," replied Wilson. "But, what are they?"

"Beats me. What kind of power does Calian have? Did he tell you Takatoka?" asked Wilson.

"Any of your guesses is as good as mine," replied Takatoka.

Suddenly the sound of a neighing horse quieted the boys and made them look around in all directions. Next, the sound of dozens of horse hoofs shook the ground causing the boys to move closer to one another.

"What's happening?" asked Wilson.

"I don't know," replied Takatoka.

On the far end of the forest, a dim light shined. There were dozens of men on horseback approaching the group. Some held long spears, other had rifles, and some had arrows.

"Holy shit! Who are those guys?" asked Tariq. But none of the boys replied. They all stood transfixed on the men approaching them on horseback.

As the men rode closer, Wilson's mouth dropped open. The riders weren't men at all. They were all replicas of Calian! The riders were much more muscular than the child and had shining eyes like cats. Some of them had scars on their faces, while others had beards. A few men looked like old versions of Calian, and some were overweight. But they all embodied Calian.

The men rode up to Calian and stopped. The leader climbed off the horse, stood in front of the boy, and stared at him. Calian remained sitting on the ground with his eyes closed, unaware of the army that stood at his feet. Suddenly the man dropped to his knees and placed his face close to the ground. The man opened his mouth and screamed –

the sound was so high-pitched that it made the boys cover their ears in agony.

"What is he doing?" asked Tariq with his ears covered. The boys watched as a gray mist poured from the creature's mouth and pushed across the forest floor. Suddenly the ground lit up.

"Oh my God!" yelled Tariq.

"Holy fucking shit!" screamed Wilson.

The boys could finally see what Calian saw. They weren't standing on grass and dirt. Instead, they all were standing on a thin glass covering that separated their world from hell. Thousands of demonic creatures scratched and clawed at one another, trying to destroy the barrier that separated their world from the children's.

"Wait!" yelled Tariq. "Look at them! They're headed back to where we just came from!"

"They're going for my parents! An underground attack!" replied Wilson.

"But they can't get through, can they?" asked Takatoka.

"No. The land is protected through and through. But if something happens that changes that, my parents will be overwhelmed," replied Wilson.

"Should we go back?" asked Tariq.

Wilson looked back at the place where they'd seen the girl. There were holes in the ground where the girl's blood spilled. Several creatures had penetrated the barrier, and they were clawing with one another, attempting to climb above ground to attack the children.

"No. We need to get Michael," replied Wilson.

Suddenly the lead warrior that Calian called raised his arm high into the air.

"Daktilega!" he barked in a metallic voice. The group of ghostly soldiers surrounding began to shriek and bang on their chests. Suddenly the men started smashing their weapons into the ground, trying to break the thin glass that separated the demons from their world.

"Hey! What the fuck are they doing?" asked Tariq with a terrified look on his face. "They're trying to let the demons out!"

Wilson began moving away from the soldiers and pulling Takatoka and Tariq. Suddenly Takatoka pulled away from Wilson.

"What about Calian? We just can't leave him here."

Tariq ran over to Calian and grabbed his shoulder. As soon as he did, the soldiers stopped banging on the ground and turned to stare at the boy. The ghostly glow of their eyes and the menacing looks on their faces terrified the boy. Unsure of what they might do to him, Tariq removed his hand from Calian's shoulder.

"Calian! Come on. We're getting out of here! Calian!" yelled Tariq as he backed away. But Calian remained sitting on the ground with his eyes closed.

Suddenly the ground began to rumble. There was an explosion that sent the boys flying in different directions. Wilson climbed to his feet and looked for the others.

"Takatoka, you okay?" he asked. Takatoka rubbed his arm and responded.

"I'm fine. Where's Tariq?"

Tariq stumbled over to Wilson and bent over out of breath.

"What the hell's going on?"

Wilson looked back to where the demonic child had been. He could only make out a lot of activity, but he could not see what was happening. Wilson tapped his eye and looked again. This time, he saw that the soldiers had managed to penetrate the barrier and killed the monsters as they climbed above ground. Like fearless warriors, they engaged the demons, slicing, decapitating, and shooting them with their guns, trying to drive them back down into the burning hole. But they were no match for the monsters. The creatures bit into the warriors' flesh like ravenous beasts, pulling them down into the pit one by one. When the soldiers were gone, dozens of the creatures climbed out of the hole and turned toward the boys.

"Hey, guys! We need to get out of here," yelled Wilson. He extended his arm into the air, picked up one of the hellish creatures, and slammed it into a group of the others, sending them sprawling.

"But how?" asked Takatoka.

"We're going to have to teleport. We don't have a choice."

"But what about Calian's arm?"

"That's just a chance we're going to need to take."

Takatoka turned to run over to Calian and was surprised to find the boy standing beside him.

"Sorry. I tried my best to fight those demons off, but there were just too many of them," Calian explained, still holding his missing, damaged arm by the wrist.

"Okay, is everyone ready?" asked Wilson. After grabbing a few more demons and tossing them away, he closed his eyes and pushed from his diaphragm. Just as he did, one of the demons jumped on Calian's back and bit into his neck. There was a flash, and the boys disappeared.

3 |

The Soldier's Secret

Michael ducked behind a large tree and lowered himself to his knees. He was exhausted. He'd been running through the dark forest for hours, trying to avoid being captured by the monsters that chased him relentlessly.

"I've got to get out of here," Michael whispered as he peered around the tree into the dark woods behind him. Although he couldn't see the glowing eyes of the beasts anymore, he could hear their growling and taunts floating through the forest as they searched for him.

"We will eat your flesh. You cannot escape. This world belongs to us, and you are ours!" one of the monsters said as it ripped a tree out of the ground and hurled it to the other side of the forest.

"You cannot escape! We will feast upon your soul!" the other two-headed creature screamed before biting a chunk of flesh out of the face of the other head attached to its body and swallowing it hungrily.

Michael was terrified. He began to try to negotiate with himself internally.

Maybe if I close my eyes, this whole thing will be just a dream. Yeah. I can just lay down in this forest, close my eyes and wake up in my bed. After all, I'm just a kid. Mr. Green doesn't want me. I'm just an innocent child.

But the sound of the creatures drawing closer to his location jolted him back to reality.

"You're near. We can smell you! Soon we're going to rip open your chest and feast on your insides!" the two-headed creature growled.

Michael took off running into the forest once more.

"Gotta keep moving," Michael whispered. "I have to make it to Wilson. He'll know what to do."

The threats from the monsters brought a newfound determination to Michael's steps. He now understood that he was not only in the battle of his life; he was in the fight *for* his life. Lying to himself about his predicament wouldn't get him out of this mess. He had to find the way out.

As he pushed through the vines and briars of the forest, a thought came to Michael.

"Grandma Noya?" Michael whispered. He was sure the voice that guided him away from Mr. Green was hers, yet he hadn't seen her.

"Maybe Grandma Noya isn't dead. Maybe she's trapped in this forest like me," he mumbled. As Michael struggled to catch his breath, he decided to risk giving away his position by calling out to her once more.

"Grandma Noya! Are you there?" he whispered as quietly as he could. Still, there was no response.

Michael sighed in frustration and continued walking. He had never felt so alone in his life. Soon Michael began thinking of his family. He was happy that his mother and father had chosen to reconcile and were together at his Great Grandfather's house. When his mother had left the family, it had been a time so empty and void of happiness that Michael had thought about running away. But when his mother returned, he began to have hope once more. He'd never admit it to anyone, but he understood the reason his mother had left. His father could be such an empty shell sometimes. The man showed little emotion.

"I wonder what Wilson is doing?" he whispered.

Michael missed his older brother the most. Michael thought about all the unnecessary clashes they had. Now he might not see him again. The thought caused Michael to become emotional, and it wasn't long before tears were streaming down his face. Still, he continued running through the forest.

Soon the rays of morning sunlight began penetrating the forest above Michael. He picked up his step, realizing he only had a limited amount of time to lose the creatures before the sun made hiding impossible. Michael made a left turn hoping the change in his path would throw the animals off his scent. As soon as he took a few steps, Michael entered a dirt pathway that led away from the forest. Nervous about where the path led yet unable to turn back, he followed the trail up a small hill and down to a small creek. Carefully, Michael crossed the stream and continued walking, seeing fewer and fewer trees. Soon he stood at the edge of the forest, looking out into an open clearing. Just as he was about to walk out of the woods, he saw something that startled him.

"Holy shit!" Michael exclaimed.

He tripped and landed on his stomach, a small grunt escaping him on impact. He immediately sprang to his feet and ran to the tree closest to him to hide. Cautiously he peeked out and watched in disbelief. Standing in the middle of the clearing was a large group of soldiers. Michael was about to turn and run away, but the fear of what he was seeing made him stay in place.

These soldiers were not like any he'd ever seen in his life. Their faces glistened in the sunshine like glass. Unlike the men that held him captive, these men weren't hiding hideous creatures beneath their skin. Michael could see through their bodies as if the men were nothing but empty shapes in the sunlight.

"Ghosts," Michael whispered to himself. A shiver crawled up his spine as he realized that the men he watched were all dead. Shivering, Michael moved from behind the tree and found a large bush to hide behind. After a few seconds, he turned to look into the black forest behind him with a fresh bout of fear. Something could sneak up behind him, and Michael wouldn't even know it.

"I've got to hide," he whispered. Michael broke several branches in the large bush and crawled inside. Although the branches slashed his face, he moved his body into the bush as much as he could. After he was comfortable, he turned his attention back to the ghosts.

The uniforms these men were wearing seemed similar – yet older. Most soldiers held old-fashioned rifles while others carried handguns in their waistbands. Some men didn't seem older than thirteen, but most men were more senior. They all wore military uniforms that seemed ancient to Michael. He thought back to when he'd gone on a field trip to see a civil war reenactment with his school. He remembered the soldiers' uniforms as they held a mock battle on the field for his class.

The ghostly soldiers stood in a circle looking at something on the ground, unaware of Michael's presence. None of them spoke, yet occasionally one turned to look at the other and whisper something that Michael couldn't hear.

"What are they saying?" whispered Michael. "What are they looking at?"

When Michael attempted to look through the ghosts, he could only see a darkened shape lying at their feet. He waited patiently for one of the men to move. But every time a soldier left an opening, another soldier blocked Michael's view. Their eyes remained locked on what lay at their feet.

Suddenly Michael heard the strong gallop of an approaching horse from the other side of the clearing. He watched in astonishment as the horse and rider appeared out of nowhere on the other side of the forest.

"Okay, soldiers! Back up!" the man on horseback instructed. Slowly, the group made room for the man, and he dismounted.

"Who killed these two?"

"I did, Captain Williams. They were tough."

"I'm sure they were. Look at these bastards' shoulders."

Michael moved to a different location to try to get a better view.

"Captain Williams, are you sure we're supposed to be doing this?" asked the soldier nearest to the Captain. "I mean, we're killing so many of these things."

Captain Williams leaned over to look at the dead creature.

"Those were the instructions from up top. This campaign is government-sanctioned. Kill as many as you can," replied Captain Williams.

"But...it just doesn't seem right," the soldier continued. "These creatures are innocent. They didn't...."

Suddenly Captain Williams grew angry.

"Private, did I hear you use the word *innocent*? Did you really say that Goddamned word?"

"I...I...."

"And what about the soldiers that lost their lives battling those Injuns? Are they innocent too?"

"Captain Williams, I didn't mean...."

"Just last week, we found a private with his throat slashed and his scalp missing. And yesterday, those same bastards overran a house, killed the husband, raped his wife, and burned the house to the goddamned ground."

"Jesus!"

"They killed their kids too. A little boy and a little girl not older than 5 or 6 got burned alive by those murderous devils. And you want to feel sorry for the son-of-a-bitches?"

"No, sir!"

"There's only one way we're going to be able to get rid of those Injun bastards, and it's by getting to what hurts them the most. We have to get rid of their food supply. It's either them or us. Now, does anyone else feel sad about the job your government sent you to do?"

One of the soldiers raised his hand.

"Excuse me, Captain Williams."

"What is it? Are you feeling remorse for our enemies too?"

"No, sir. It's not that."

"Then what is it, Private? Speak!"

The soldier pointed towards the ground.

"One of the animals...it's still alive."

The group took a step back, which allowed Michael to see what lay at the soldier's feet. What he saw made Michael want to scream. He quickly covered his mouth and started trembling uncontrollably. Laying in the center of the group of men were the bodies of Michael and his brother older brother Wilson. They both appeared to be dead.

Michael inspected the two bodies while they lay in the dirt and felt a sickness in his stomach that he'd never felt. He stared at his own body and wanted to puke. His face was pale and lifeless, a faraway gaze in his open eyes. He was dead; the deep gash on his throat and the bullet wound to the side of his skull proved it.

"Those motherfuckers!" Michael whispered as he looked at his dead body from the shadows of the forest.

Wilson's head lay on his brother's stomach, a pathetic look on his face. He had several bullet holes in the center of his chest with large purple bruises all over his body. Thick white drool ran out of the corner of his mouth and pooled on his brother's belly as the boy made gravelly noises trying to suck in a breath. The sight of his brother's pitiful state made Michael cry as he watched, unable to do or say anything to intervene.

"They tortured him," whispered Michael from the forest. "Wilson..."

Captain Williams walked over to Wilson and placed his boot firmly on the boy's chest.

"Private Jenkins, give me your knife."

One of the soldiers passed a large brown leather bag to the man, and he unsheathed a large knife from inside the case. Captain Williams leaned over and placed the blade on Wilson's throat. As he did so, he spoke:

"We can't be afraid of our duties, boys. Underestimate the enemy's strength at your peril. These savages are cunning - pure evil. Weakness means certain death at their hands. We have to cleanse this country so that the Christian way of life can move forward. It's all preordained. This country is ours, not theirs! We have to irradicate these savages by killing their animals. It's the only way."

And with those words, Captain Williams ran the blade across Wilson's throat. Michael sobbed as he watched a large gash appear in his brother's neck. The boy began gasping for air as blood blanketed his chest like crimson paint. Just as Wilson's eyes started rolling back in his head, Captain Williams drew a pistol from his waist, cocked it, and shot the boy in his temple.

4

Mom and Dad

Dustin woke up and yanked the covers off his sweaty naked body.

"Julia?" he asked while looking around the bedroom for his wife. "Where are you?"

Dustin climbed out of bed, grabbed the rubber band on the nightstand, and wrapped his long black hair in a bun. After smacking at a few mosquitos, he forwent his clothing and walked to the living room. The front door was open, and Dustin saw a figure sitting on the edge of the porch with a sheet draped over her shoulders.

"Julia?"

Julia turned around and smiled at Wilson.

"I couldn't sleep. It's so fucking hot in there."

"I couldn't sleep either."

Dustin sat his naked butt down on the wooden porch, and Julia snickered.

"You sure you don't want to put on some boxers? This porch is full of splinters."

"I'll be okay. It's cooler without clothes."

Julia turned away and continued staring down at the ground.

"You're thinking about the boys, huh? I'm sure they're fine."

Julia gave a half-hearted smile and nodded in the direction of the forest.

"It's hard not to think of the boys when this madness surrounds us," replied Julia pointing towards the forest. "Look. More showed up."

Dustin looked out towards the edge of the yard and shifted uncomfortably on the porch. He couldn't hide the uneasiness he felt in what he saw. Although the forest was pitch black, he could see thousands of glowing eyes staring at them from the shadows. Indeed, it seemed that more demons had arrived than when they'd gone to sleep the previous evening. Dustin wiped the sleep from his eyes and sighed. He didn't know how to tell his wife that he was terrified.

Suddenly, a loud, deep bellow rose from the forest's darkness. The sound was so evil that Julia became afraid and moved close to Dustin.

"Dustin, what's happening?" she asked, shaking in fear.

They both watched in horror as two gigantic claws extended from the darkness, grabbed two tall oak trees, and ripped them out of the earth. The two trees hovered midair for a few moments before a humungous hideous lizard-like face appeared. The monster inspected the trees, opened his vast mouth, and bit them, splitting them in two. The creature's glowing red eyes saw the couple sitting on the front porch and let out another scream before rushing toward the two lovers. As soon as the beast attempted to run onto the sacred land, several blue bolts of electricity flashed and vaporized the monster.

Julia's tense body relaxed in her husband's arms. Dustin rubbed her back and tried to comfort his wife.

"We're safe, Julia. No need to worry."

Julia pushed Dustin's hands away and stood up.

"We're safe? Great! But what about our sons? What about Wilson and Michael? How can you sit there and accept what we just saw without being terrified for our sons? Don't you care that our children are in danger?"

Dustin stood and looked out into the forest.

"The attempted crossings are becoming more frequent. That blue flash used to appear once a day, and now it's flashing two or three times every hour," said Dustin.

"Don't you fucking ignore me, Dustin! What about our kids?"

Dustin scratched his genitals and walked to the front door.

"They'll be fine. Mother taught them well."

"Who? Grandma Noya?! She's fucking dead!"

Julia's words made Dustin angry, and he turned to yell at her. But after seeing the pain and fear in her eyes, Dustin suddenly backed down. After remaining silent for a few seconds, Dustin spoke to her calmly. Although he didn't like the tone of her words, he understood his wife's emotions - they were the fears of a mother.

"Mom isn't dead. She's just on a different path."

This statement sent Julia into a rage. She had hoped to provoke Dustin with the comment about his mother. But instead, what she got was a pseudo-Zen-like response that reminded her of why she abandoned her husband in the first place.

"You see? That's why I left! You haven't changed one bit! Instead of dealing with reality, you go off on some weird tangent about the afterlife. We're here! In this life! And our sons are out there alone!"

Dustin slapped his arms and legs.

"I guess I'd better go and put on some pants. These mosquitos are eating me alive."

Dustin turned away from his wife and walked into the house. As soon as he was gone, Julia covered her face with the bedsheet and sobbed.

"Sometimes..." a child's voice spoke out.

Julia jumped at the sound of the voice and recoiled to the edge of the porch. Sitting in the rocking chair on the other side of the porch was the ghost of a shirtless little Black boy in ragged shorts.

"Sometimes, mom asks me to go out to work in the fields with Uncle Buck and Jimmy."

Julia looked away from the ghost towards the dark field. She didn't care how much Dustin tried to explain to her how the spirits were good. Julia could never get used to them appearing at random. She didn't tell Dustin about it, but while they were making love, she'd seen the ghost of an elderly man walk past the room. Julia had jumped when she saw the spirit, but Dustin never noticed because he was on top of her.

"I never wanted to go out into the fields to work," the child continued.

Julia decided to humor herself by responding.

"You never wanted to go? Then why did you?"

"Mom told me there are some things that are a matter of duty and responsibility."

Julia bit her arm in frustration.

"Are you saying Michael and Wilson are out there because of their responsibilities?"

The little boy stood and stepped off the porch into the front yard.

"After Dad was shot and hanged in the pasture, Mom didn't want me to stay home. She knew she couldn't teach me how to be a man, so she sent me out in the fields to work with Uncle Buck. She always told me being out there sweating in the sun would teach me how to survive. But it didn't help. Not in the way she hoped. When I went out there sweating in the weeds working with my uncle, I lost my childhood. I stopped seeing through the hopeful eyes of a child. I had to become a cold man much too soon. And now...."

Julia grew frustrated. Was this what Dustin was trying to do with Wilson and Michael? She began combing through their interactions for answers. Dustin always treated the boys like they were adults, completely ignoring the fact they were his young sons. He never spent time with them. Whether playing video games or going camping, Dustin was always absent in their lives. Was this Dustin's plan to force the boys into adulthood and absolve himself of parental responsibility?

Bored with the indirect conversation she was having with the ghost-child, Julia stood to go back into the house.

"There are secrets about our family my mom should've told me," the boy continued. "Just as there are secrets your husband hasn't told you."

Julia turned to face the child again.

"Secrets? What secrets?" she asked, staring directly at the boy.

He smiled.

"I found the book, and then I understood. The book has all the answers."

"What book?"

The child ignored her and continued talking.

"I'm not supposed to know how to read, but Mom made sure to teach June and me. We keep it a secret. That's what Mom said. We have to keep it a secret. Mom told me if anyone finds out that we can read, they will kill us. It's the law. No Black person is allowed to read."

Frustrated, Julia questioned the boy more forcefully.

"Look! What book are you talking about?"

"Mom told us about a family like ours on the other side of town where the White men found out they could read, and they killed everyone in the house. At least that's what Mom told us."

Julia remained silent as she watched the ghostly child staring into the woods.

"Things are getting worse, but you'll be okay. Look under the bed. The book is there."

The child turned as if he heard something and cupped his hands around his mouth.

"What? Is dinner almost ready? Yes ma'am. I'm coming."

Julia didn't hear anyone calling the child.

Suddenly the boy took off running and melted away into the night.

5

Darkened Travels

Wilson froze in place and didn't move until he started seeing shapes within the whiteness that temporarily blinded him. Soon he could make out the pile of burning wood and chunks of concrete that used to be his Grandma Noya's house. As more of the burned house came into view, Wilson started feeling a deep pain in his chest. The memories of the summers he and his little brother spent playing in Grandma Noya's yard and exploring the forest rushed his senses like a tidal wave. Wilson felt the urge to cry but pushed the desire deep down inside. He couldn't let the boys see him crying. Not now.

Suddenly his eyes fell on a deflated half-melted basketball with string around it. Wilson smiled and lifted the charred orange ball of rubber from the ground.

"I tried, Grandma Noya. I did," he whispered as he remembered one of the worst days of his childhood. He remembered how he had begged his Grandma for a football – after she had only a few months earlier given him the basketball. Grandma Noya immediately denied his new request.

"Just a few months ago, you asked me for a basketball. You were supposed to try out for the basketball team. What happened?" Grandma Noya had asked him.

"I didn't make it." Wilson had confessed.

"So just because you fail at something, you give up? Just like that? That is not the way the world works."

"Please, Grandma Noya. If you buy me a new football, I promise I won't ask you for anything else."

"If you want to play football, you're going to have to convince me that you're serious before I throw money away behind your dreams again."

"But it's not a dream. It's a...."

"Look, child. I have pigs to slop. You want to help?"

Angry that his grandmother refused to buy him a football, Wilson stormed into the kitchen and grabbed a knife. He walked out of the house, sat down on the front porch, and plunged the knife into the basketball.

"I'll show her," he mumbled as he tried to prove his seriousness. Wilson destroyed the gift Grandmother Noya had given him and created a makeshift football in hopes of convincing her that he was serious. But when she saw how little he cared about the gift she'd given him, all it did was hurt her feelings.

Wilson sighed. There were so many things he never got the opportunity to tell Grandma Noya. And now his grandmother was gone. And no matter what he did, there was nothing Wilson could do to bring her back.

Filled with regret, he tossed the ball of rubber into the weeds. Slowly he turned away from the rubble and looked across the street at his other relative's house, Nana Ama's. Her home, too, was destroyed while the fires continued to burn in the forest just behind the demolished structure – where Wilson first saw the hell living in her backyard. Wilson licked his lips and swallowed hard – the onion smell he'd smelled when he previously transported his family was back, along with the tremendous urge to spray what little food he had left in his stomach all over the ground.

"Shit, dude. Traveling this way fucking sucks," Wilson heard a voice complain to his left. He looked over and saw Tariq doubled over, holding his stomach.

"What the heck is that smell?" asked Takatoka.

"Burned onions. It happens during the process. I don't know why," explained Wilson.

Takatoka shook his head in disagreement.

"No. That's not it. It's something else."

Wilson breathed again. Takatoka was right. The smell was worse than the burned onion smell he detected when he teleported his family for the first time. This smell was different – it smelled like death. As Wilson surveyed the area to see where they were, he was startled when Tariq yelled.

"Holy fucking Christ!" Tariq screamed.

Wilson turned to see Tariq on the ground, backpedaling on his palms away from the group, his eyes focused on what was behind Wilson. Slowly, Wilson turned and saw Calian lying on his back.

Calian's eyes were wide open, but Wilson could tell he was unconscious. A faraway look was frozen on his face that scared Wilson to his core. Calian's unblinking eyes stared up into nothingness as if he had seen something so terrifying that it had snatched the life out of his body. Blood dripped from the corners of Calian's eyes while a pink foam bubbled out of his mouth.

"Oh my God!" whispered Wilson.

Attached to Calian's neck was the head of one of the demons from the forest; its teeth were burrowed deep into the boy's flesh; its solid white colorless eyes were open, fixated on Calian's face. Wilson moved in closer for a better look. The creature's pale skin was oily and seemed to be sweating. Afraid that the monster was still alive, Wilson covered his nose and backed away. The smell of death seemed to be coming from the creature.

"Is it alive?" asked Tariq, finally on his feet again. He moved in behind Wilson and stared over his shoulder. Wilson nudged Tariq back from the creature, afraid of what powers the creature still possessed even though it was decapitated.

"Where's the body?" asked Tariq. Suddenly the boys became nervous. All three of them scanned the ground anxiously, looking for the monster's body. Unable to find the corpse, a terrifying thought came into Wilson's mind. Frantically he started inspecting his body for signs that something may have attached to him during their teleportation. Tariq noticed Wilson touching his neck and running his hands over his body.

"What? You think something could've gotten us too?" asked Tariq with wide eyes. Soon all three boys were rubbing their bodies, searching for anything out of the ordinary.

"I knew this would turn out bad," complained Takatoka. "I should've ignored Granddad and stayed at home."

Satisfied that nothing had infected his body, Wilson turned his attention back to Calian.

"Calian! You awake?" Wilson asked. He couldn't see signs of life from Calian; his chest wasn't moving up and down, and the boy continued lying motionless. Wilson grabbed a stick from the ground and swatted at the head of the demon. Several chunks of pale flesh fell from its face revealing a shiny black skull beneath the flesh.

"Oh my God! That's fucking gross!" yelled Tariq. "Get it off of him!"

Wilson swatted at the head once more, and the skull cracked open. Although he was disgusted by the creature's appearance, Wilson was surprised at how soft the dome of the beast was. Hitting the monster's head with the stick felt like swatting a firm pillow. Wilson hit the skull again, and the creature's jaw popped open and rolled away from Calian.

"I think I'm going to be sick!" yelled Takatoka. Wilson looked at Calian's neck, and he also felt the urge to vomit. Over forty bite marks, each hole was leaking a thick clear fluid.

Tariq backed away.

"Um...Wilson," Tariq whispered.

"Yeah?" asked Wilson, unable to move his eyes from the monster's skull.

"Get back."

"What?"

"Move away from Calian."

The statement caught Wilson's attention, and he looked at Tariq. Slowly, his eyes traced to where Tariq was staring, and he jumped in surprise. Calian was no longer missing a hand.

"Didn't Calian have his hand bitten off?" asked Tariq.

"Yeah," Wilson responded.

"Then what the fuck...."

Takaoka's eyes finally fell on what the boys were watching.

"Oh my God!" Takatoka whispered.

An arm much more protracted than Calian's original appendage had grown from the open wound the boy had. Instead of a human hand, there was a long puffy leathery claw with eight thick fingers and sharp black nails extending from the fingertips. The top of the hand moved as though something was inside, trying to free itself.

"Come on, let's go," said Wilson.

"You're just going to leave him here? Something's inside of him. At the very least, we need to put him out of his misery," exclaimed Takatoka.

"Are you going to do it?" asked Tariq, backing away.

Takatoka looked at Calian again.

"No...I mean, we all have to. Don't we?"

Tariq shot a nervous look at Wilson.

Suddenly there was a giant whoosh of air from Calian's mouth, and he sat up.

"Help...Help me. It hurts," Calian said in a garbled phlegm-filled voice. Calian lifted his long mutant arm and extended it to the boys.

"T...Tariq. You have to help me," Calian begged.

Takatoka pushed Tariq.

"Do something!"

Tariq recoiled when he saw the pulsating arm reaching for him.

"Fuck you! I'm not touching him! You do it!"

The long, extended arm Calian held out began to shake violently, thrashing the boy continuously into the ground like a rag doll.

"Please!" Calian yelled. "Somebody do something! It hurts!"

"Wilson! You've got to do something!" begged Tariq.

Wilson touched his eye and was about to reach out to grab Calian when he saw what was really inside the boy's arm – dozens of hatching eggs filled with hungry worms that chewed on the boy's flesh as they were released.

"Let's go! Now!" yelled Wilson as he moved in a large arch around Calian. Tariq didn't complain and moved in the same path as Wilson.

"But...we just can't leave him," protested Takatoka.

Suddenly Calian stopped thrashing on the ground and rose slowly to his feet. Takatoka was about to run but could not remove his eyes from his friend.

"Calian, are you okay?" Takatoka asked, looking for familiar signs of life in the boy he once knew.

"Nobody's going anywhere!" Calian hissed, his voice sounding like he was speaking with three demonic voices at once. Wilson continued moving away from the boy while speaking.

"Takatoka. Now's your only chance. Run!"

Like Tariq and Wilson, Takatoka sprinted around the injured boy. Calian's eyes started pouring a black liquid, and he started laughing uncontrollably.

"Do you think you can escape us? No one escapes the delicious pain of hell. He eventually comes for us all."

Wilson ignored Calian's words and continued moving away from the boy.

"Just keep moving. Don't stop."

Suddenly Calian lifted his grotesque arm to his mouth and bit into the vein-filled flesh. Blood squirted in all directions, and hundreds of worms fell to the ground. Calian opened his mouth once more, bit one of the claw-like fingers off, and swallowed it without chewing.

"Help me, Wilson. I'm so hungry," Calian cried in a childlike voice. Soon worms started pouring out of the hand and crawling on Calian's face. The horrific sight so shook Wilson that he took a step in Calian's direction, searching for a way to help the boy. But after realizing that Calian was beyond help, Wilson pulled himself back and watched in disgust as hundreds of worms stuffed the child's nose, eyes, mouth, and ears, causing the boy to reach out for help with worm-covered swinging arms.

"Let's go!" yelled Wilson and took off sprinting in the direction of his Great Grandmother Ama's house. The two other boys followed without looking back at Calian.

"You can't get away!" Calian's voice echoed. "This is our world!"

Within seconds Wilson made it out of the forest and to the road. Suddenly there came a deep rumbling from overhead. Wilson looked up to see immense black clouds growing in the sky. Determined to get as far away from Calian as possible, Wilson ignored the clouds and continued walking towards his great-grandmother's house. Suddenly a bolt of lightning struck the forest where the trio had been standing.

"Shit!" yelled Tariq.

"We'd better hurry up and find some cover before it starts raining," said Wilson as he picked up his pace. Suddenly the clouds unleashed multiple lightning bolts at once, and they all struck the area where Calian was. Wilson was about to make a run for shelter when three more lightning strikes hit the same place again.

"My God!" yelled Takatoka. The boys stopped, turned around to watch in shock as lightning continuously struck again and again and again. After a while, the lightning stopped, and everything was silent. Soon a familiar faraway voice rose in the night air.

"Wilson! Tariq! Takatoka!" the voice cried. The boys' eyes widened as they stared at one another in disbelief.

"Don't leave me," the voice continued. "Please! It hurts so much! You've got to help me."

Wilson was about to tap his eye to put Calian out of his misery but stopped suddenly. Takatoka noticed his delay.

"What are you waiting for?"

"I don't know. I just feel like it's a setup."

"How?"

"That's not Calian. Someone is controlling him."

"Yeah? Who? That guy Mr. Green?"

"It could be him.... or something else. Whoever or whatever it is, it feels like a trap."

Tariq agreed.

"Yeah. It feels like that to me too."

Takatoka disagreed with the boys.

"Am I the only person that saw those worms? And what about the lightning strikes? Maybe he's asking for help because he's really hurt."

Tariq shrugged.

"When I went hunting with my granddad, one of the cruelest things he ever did was to leave an animal stuck in one of his animal traps."

Frustrated, Takatoka rolled his eyes.

"What does that have to do with this?"

"Calian may be the animal in the trap. And whoever is on the other end of setting that trap may be calling us in through Calian's pain."

"What if that were you out there, Tariq? Wouldn't you want us to put you out of your misery if you were going through such a thing?"

"Maybe. But I damn sure wouldn't want you to come back and risk your life and fall victim to a plan to entrap us all."

Several more lightning bolts struck the area where the boys had last seen Calian, and a scream rose into the dark sky.

"Was that Calian?" asked Tariq. Wilson didn't bother answering. He knew the answer, and he wanted to get away from the area as quickly as possible.

"Come on. Let's get out of here," said Wilson as he started jogging towards the place where his Great Grandmother's house had been. Tariq and Takatoka followed. As the boys climbed the mound of dirt leading to Wilson's Great Grandmother's house, a loud commotion rose from the forest behind them. The group stopped and turned to look back. The three boys watched in amazement as the giant trees swayed back and forth as if shaken by a giant. Soon the sounds of wild animals became clearer.

"Wolves?" Tariq asked.

"Are you crazy? Look at the way those trees are moving," responded Takatoka.

"Wait! You hear that?" asked Wilson.

The other boys stopped talking and listened intently. In the middle of the growling and aggression of the creatures in the forest was a child's laughter.

"What is that?" asked Takatoka.

"It's Calian, I think. He's laughing," Wilson responded.

"Did hell take him? Is he one of them?" asked Tariq.

"Yes," replied Wilson as he turned away from the noise and started jogging again. Tariq and Takatoka followed him.

6 |

The Trap

Michael stayed hidden. His mom had told him that ghosts were only a figment of his imagination, but here he was watching them, their existence visually confirmed and undeniable. A strange inconsistency struck Michael in what he was watching. In the horror movies Michael watched with his brother, ghosts seemed to glide easily, floating through the air as if propelled by some magical force. But not these ghosts. These things didn't move in concert with the fears chewing at Michael's insides as he watched from the shadows. They were as clumsy as the people in real life and struggled with maintaining balance. Their clothing was imperfect, and their movements were as stiff as hangers in a closet. They weren't glamourous, and there didn't seem to be anything mystical about them. To Michael, the creatures reeked of familiarity. Michael closed his mouth and took in a breath of air through his nose. The army of ghosts had the same smell as some of the things he most hated in life: the rotting tires on his uncle's broken-down station wagon parked in the back of Grandma Noya's house; the disgusting smell of low-budget food coming from the cafeteria in school; the "old people smell" of his teacher's dentures when he went to her desk to ask for help on a math problem.

Still, Michael couldn't deny what he was watching. Aside from the specifics his nose told him, his eyes told him these things were real. He had to assume the worst about their capabilities. They could kill him.

Based on what he saw before his very eyes, they *had* killed him and would probably do it again if they found him.

And then it happened—the repeat.

There was a flash of blinding light, and the ghostly soldiers all returned to their original positions, standing in a circle blocking Michael's view from what they all were watching. Within a few seconds, the trees across the field shivered, and the same rider on horseback galloped out of the forest's darkness. The sight of the rider made Michael's blood boil, and he fought to contain his vengeful desires. Seeing the same scene play out for a second time proved to be no less infuriating and made Michael fantasize about what he would do – if it were possible to kill ghosts. Still, Michael kept his anger in check and watched in silence from the shadows. He watched as the man gave the same lame speech to motivate the dumb soldiers who only minimally questioned their evil objectives. Michael watched as the men accepted what their leader told them for a second time.

Eventually, the men moved to allow Michael to view once again what was at the ghastly center of their circle – two young boys, one dead and the other clinging to life, Michael and his brother Wilson.

Michael filled his lungs with another deep breath and held it, just long enough to look at the faces of each of the men to see their reactions. One baby-faced man looked away, disturbed by the sight of death and unable to hide his displeasure in seeing such a horrible thing. Another soldier seemed to be excited by what was transpiring in his presence. He shifted anxiously back and forth while stroking the butt of his rifle as if it were the arm of his girlfriend, a strange smile on his face.

Michael let out his breath slowly and quietly while running his fingers along his arm to remind himself he was still alive. Once again, Michael saw his brother Wilson gasping for air, but he watched his brother closely this time. Although Wilson *looked* like his brother, Michael couldn't get over how much Wilson *didn't* resemble the boy who slept beside him in their shared bedroom at home. There was something so strange about the mannerisms of the boy. For instance, although his brother lay dead beneath him, not once did Wilson look at Michael's corpse. Not once. From everything that Michael knew of his brother, they loved one another fiercely. Not seeing Wilson acknowledge what the men had done to Michael seemed strangely out of place.

Another thing that Michael noticed was the absence of fight in his brother's behavior. Sure, there was emotion on Wilson's face, but the boy that lay in that circle seemed indifferent even to put up a struggle. The sight of Wilson's presence made Michael rack his brain in frustration. Why was Wilson behaving so uncharacteristically? Suddenly a thought came into Michael's head, and his eyes lit up. The look on Wilson's face – he'd seen it before. Michael had seen it when he went deer hunting with his uncle in the forest behind Grandma Noya's house: the watery eyes that seemed on the verge of crying; the dry, foamy mouth; the uncontrollable body spasms. Michael had seen it all in the eyes of the deer as it lay beneath his uncle's hunting knife.

When the time came for the slaughtering of Wilson, Michael was so sure that what he was watching *wasn't* the murder of his brother that he was almost totally divorced from the idea. The wet slimy sound of the sharp blade as the man ran it across Wilson's neck was upsetting, but not as much as before. Michael was sure he wasn't watching his older brother's murder and could live with what he was watching.

And then it happened - again. And then again. And again.

Michael sat in the bushes watching the ghosts of the soldiers for hours. He held his position from the dark shadows and remained quiet. Over and over, he watched as the same ghostly scene played in a continuous loop - soldiers standing in a circle over Michael and Wilson; the eventual arrival of the man on horseback who emerged from the forest to give his speech and then cut Wilson's throat before shooting a bullet into his head.

After seeing the same scene play for the third and fourth time in the setting sun, Michael realized that the scene seemed to be a recording of some kind, a visual marker of an important event that had happened – or was about to.

By the time the last rays of the sun crawled across the grass and disappeared, Michael could barely see the ghosts. Everything gradually melted away when the stars appeared in the sky.

After checking to ensure no hideous monsters were watching him, Michael crawled out from his hiding space and stood up in the forest. The air was chilly and made him wish he had a jacket. His bottom lip began to tremble, and Michael wrapped his tiny arms around his torso. He paused to stare at the bushes directly across from him – the place where he'd seen the man on horseback emerge repeatedly. Although nothing was there, Michael was hesitant to move forward. Slowly, his eyes fell on the place where his dead body had been, the place where he'd seen his brother murdered. Suddenly a thought came into the child's head that genuinely terrified him.

"Am I dead or alive?" he whispered. "Am I a ghost?"

Fear crawled across Michael's back like dozens of spiders made of ice. After all that had happened with him and the monsters in the forest, it was possible that he was already dead and didn't realize it. How else could he explain seeing his own dead body? This thought pushed Michael over the edge, and he started shivering uncontrollably.

"Come on, Mike. You're not dead," he whispered as he cupped his palms and blew into them for warmth. After a few moments, he tried to steady himself with memories of what Grandma Noya had told him when he and his brother were training. His grandmother had made Michael and Wilson memorize the words and recite them to her every night:

"You can't be afraid of this world because it's not the end. Although death comes to all, it isn't final. Life continues whether we choose to believe or not," Michael whispered to himself, trying desperately to strengthen his nerves. Still, Michael *was* afraid. He'd seen his own death. Things like that weren't supposed to exist, and no one was there to explain things to him. At that moment, he truly felt like what he was, a lost kid in an evil world.

Michael looked around once more and stepped out onto the open field. He immediately saw a tall shadowy figure standing at the far end of the area just as he did. Michael attempted to pull himself back into hiding, but it was too late. His feet had carried him beyond his hiding spot, and he stood exposed to whatever was watching him. Remembering Grandma Noya's teaching, Michael stared directly at the creature and tried to suppress his fear. He began to tremble as the figure returned the stare, unflinching in its piercing gaze. Although Michael couldn't see the being's face hidden beneath the long black shroud it wore, he could see the creature's other characteristics; it had long arms, legs, and a head. Yet, to Michael, the being was too strange to be an actual person. It was as tall as a tree, and its arms were so thin that Michael doubted the creature could lift them.

"When he comes," an icy voice whispered across the field.

Michael tried to run but found that his legs were too weak to carry him. He fell backward and landed on his butt, unable to take his eyes off the shadow that was watching him.

"When he comes," the voice repeated.

Michael felt paralyzed. He couldn't move beyond the sitting position in which he'd landed. Something was holding him in place. He struggled unsuccessfully a few more times to get up but relented and began to cry.

"When he comes," the creature whispered again.

Michael blinked through tears and tried his best to hide his fear.

"What do you want, you son of a bitch?" Michael snapped. He was surprised at how good cursing felt, and he felt some of the fear melt away.

"When he comes," the creature repeated.

"When who comes?" Michael yelled angrily across the field. "Who? Mr. Green? Fuck that bitch!"

Michael knew he shouldn't agitate the creature, but he was tired of feeling like a lost child in this strange place. He felt like fighting back.

Still, the creature didn't respond. Its disregard for Michael's question angered the boy even more.

"You're a pussy. Do you know that? What kind of creature takes advantage of a kid? You sorry sack of shit!"

There was a rustling of leaves and the sound of tree limbs snapping. Slowly the creature walked out onto the open field and moved towards the child. Michael finally saw the beast entirely, and his eyes widened. The *thing* was faceless – that's what Michael decided to call it internally, a *"thing"* because he didn't have the words to describe what it was. Michael gasped in surprise as the creature extended its two long arms and grabbed onto trees on either side of the clearing to steady itself as it moved in slow motion across the field. Michael could hear the thing taking in a breath like a long rush of wind blowing through a cave and then exhaling in a deep humming sound.

Suddenly the creature stopped. It swayed back and forth before finally releasing its hold on the trees. Michael jumped as a loud popping noise seemed to come from all directions. He looked around to see if other monsters were approaching but saw none. When he turned his attention back to the creature standing on the other side of the field, he almost fainted. Walking towards him was an enormous buffalo, its throat cut and blood spraying out of the gaping wound in its neck.

"When he comes..." the voice repeated.

Michael heard the popping noise again, but he didn't remove his attention from the buffalo walking towards him this time. He watched in astonishment as the buffalo melted away right before his eyes, and the original shadowy creature reappeared.

"When who comes?" Michael bravely asked.

Suddenly the creature stopped and opened its black robe to reveal a thin black shadow. It tossed the robe into the forest, and a large hole appeared on the ground where the robe landed, sucking in several plants and trees.

Michael's mouth fell open as the monster transformed again. But this time, Michael saw stretching skin, flesh, bones, and organs materialize out of the blackness as though something was ripped apart and pieced together by some unknown force. By the time the transformation was complete, a huge lion was staring at the child in the field. Michael could feel the heat of its breath warming his face from a distance. Suddenly the main of the lion burst into flame, and it lifted its gigantic head to scream out in agony. But instead of a thunderous roar, Michael heard the screams of children fill the night air. The lion took several steps toward Michael and opened its enormous mouth again. This time Michael stopped breathing. Deep within the lion's mouth were the arms of children, all seemingly alive and clamoring at the corners of the animal's mouth as they tried to escape.

"Oh my God! Please! Don't kill me!" Michael whimpered. The lion glared at Michael and took another step in his direction. Michael closed his eyes and urinated on himself.

"Stop! Please! I'm sorry! Please!" the small boy yelled.

The creature paused and transformed back to its original shadowy form. Soon it took another step and changed into a Cherokee warrior. Michael screamed when he saw the warrior's face - it was half his father and half his brother Wilson's, their faces stitched together on one body. There were large holes in the warrior's chest, and Michael could see a red heart beating.

"The day of reckoning is upon you," the creature continued.

"I...don't know what that means," exclaimed Michael as he shook uncontrollably.

"Fear is of no consequence. Retribution will begin at his arrival."

Suddenly there was a flash of light, and then the creature was gone.

Michael wiped his eyes and attempted to stand up but was surprised to find that he still could not move.

"What...is.... this?" he asked as he struggled to free himself. "Somebody, please help!"

But there was no response. There was only the coldness of the night and the racing heart of a child battling fear and loneliness in the center of an empty field. Soon Michael heard strange sounds in the forests all around him. His eyes darted from left to right as he scanned the woods, trying to see what hellish creature would come to kill him. He knew Mr. Green was probably somewhere in the darkness lurking, wanting to burn him just as Michael had done with the triangle.

Suddenly Michael's eyes lit up.

The triangle!

Michael tried to move his left hand to his hip but found that he couldn't do it.

"Fuck!" he yelled. He tried to move his right hand, but it also was frozen as if some magical power had it plastered against the soil. His heart was beating so fast that Michael started having trouble breathing. Soon he was gasping as he tried to get to the one weapon that had saved him from death earlier. He began to see floaters in his vision as he continued to struggle to break free.

"Come on! Let me go!" he yelled. Suddenly he stopped moving and stared into the forest. Michael could see dozens of glowing eyes peering at him from the woods, growling and whispering his name.

"We see you. The sweetness of your flesh draws us near."

"You cannot escape us, child. We smell your fear."

Michael's heart sank. It was the same voices from the creatures who were after him earlier. Michael struggled anew to free himself, but the power of what was about to happen to him was too much for his young heart. Within minutes his desperation drained all his energy, and drowsiness began to take hold. Soon he stopped struggling altogether.

"I don't care anymore," Michael said as he accepted the fatigue without struggle. "Maybe death won't be so bad," he whispered. He began to allow supposition to relax him.

"Grandma Noya's dead. Mom and Dad are probably dead too. Wilson's probably dead too. There's no way he'd be able to make it alone. I may as well join them."

Michael looked into the forests and saw several bushes shaking. He knew what was there, but he didn't care.

"Just come get me and get it over with," he yelled.

But the creatures never attacked. They remained hidden, and Michael remained contained in the middle of the field by some unknown force. Soon Michael's head began to droop, and he smiled as a thought came into his head.

"I know you're protecting me, Grandma Noya," he whispered.

Just as he was about to pass out, Mr. Green appeared at the edge of the field. An evil grimace was on his face, and his eyes glowed red as he watched the child.

"I knew you would come for me," whispered Michael before finally losing consciousness. Mr. Green smiled and turned away from the boy and walked back into the forest.

7

Every Family Has Secrets

It was noon when Dustin walked off the porch and into the back-yard. Julia walked out of the backdoor and followed him.

"Do you have to go now?" Julia asked as Dustin grabbed the tin bucket from the side of the porch and headed towards the tall weeds.

"Don't start, Julia. You know the routine. Are we supposed to die of thirst?"

"I know, but.... you're leaving me all alone."

Dustin paused and exhaled a breath in frustration.

"The spirits are harmless. How many times do I have to...?"

"You know it's not only the ghosts. We haven't heard from the boys since that man took Michael."

"Wilson will get him back. You'll see. Mom trained them well."

"About that training...."

"Here we go again."

"Yes, Dustin. Here we go again. On top of lying to me about your mother's true intentions, you refuse to tell me the truth about your family's history."

"I've told you!"

"You've told me? Told me what? You've only given me pieces of the truth!"

Dustin slammed the bucket on the ground.

"Damn it, Julia! I have to make this trip back and forth eleven times to get enough water. Unless you want to go out into the weeds to take a shit tonight, I suggest you let me get enough water to pour down the toilet for the flush!"

They were out of water again, and Julia knew Dustin had to go to the well. Still, there were so many things that Dustin hadn't answered, and it was beyond time for her husband to come clean about it all. As far as Julia was concerned, Dustin's family secrets may have contributed to the death of their son.

After glaring at Dustin, Julia relented.

"Fine. Go. But this isn't over."

Dustin snatched the bucket from the ground and mumbled under his breath in Cherokee before disappearing into the tall grass. Julia's eyes filled with tears as the sound of her husband pushing through the weeds became faint.

"I can't take much more of this shit!" she yelled behind him. Dustin didn't respond.

"Selfish prick!" Julia snapped.

It had been days since her youngest son Michael got abducted by the strange man at the edge of the forest, and Dustin didn't seem bothered by the absence of his sons. In fact, with each trip Dustin made to get water from the well, he spoke less and less about the children.

Suddenly a cold breeze brushed past Julia, chilling her to the bone. She folded her arms and shivered. Finally, she remembered what Dustin had previously explained to her:

"Whenever you feel a gust of cold air, a spirit has passed through you to get to their destination."

Julia looked around the yard and didn't see anything. Finally, she turned and looked behind her. Standing just outside the screen door was the ghost of a chubby elderly Black woman. There was a long scar that stretched from the woman's scalp, through her white blind eye, and down her chin. Julia didn't look away. Instead, she watched the woman intently. The old woman stooped and picked up something from the ground. After a few seconds, the ghost stared directly at Julia and smiled. Julia smiled back.

"I must be losing my mind if I'm getting used to this shit," Julia whispered. If she had seen a ghost with such a horrific injury when she and Dustin first arrived, the sight would've sent Julia into panic mode. But after Dustin explained that most of the spirits had been victims subjected to torture by their captors, Julia confronted her fear. It wasn't long before she realized that many of the souls still roaming about had probably been murdered. Finally, guilt began tugging at her heart. There was no doubt in her mind that someone that looked like her had harmed these people. After going through many emotional twists and turns, Julia stopped being afraid.

Suddenly the ghost of a little girl came sprinting from around the house and ran up to the old woman. The child wrapped her arms around the old woman's waist, and they both started walking towards the back door. Suddenly they both stopped. The little girl turned back to wave at Julia. Surprised by the sweet gesture, Julia waved and flashed a brighter smile. The old woman kissed the child on the forehead, and they both walked through the door without opening it, disappearing into the house.

After the woman and child disappeared, Julia's anger returned, and she turned to glare into the weeds. Soon feelings of resentment overcame Julia, and numerous questions filled her head.

Why did she now have the feeling that her husband knew more about the strange man than he let on? Could she even trust Dustin anymore? How could she let Dustin talk her into allowing Wilson, a boy not yet a teenager, into going into a forest filled with evil? Why didn't Dustin accept his position as father and own up to that responsibility? A father was supposed to protect his sons. The sons weren't supposed to be protecting the father.

"I should've left his ass," she whispered. "I was almost out the door. Why did I come back?"

She knew something wasn't right about Dustin and his family from the start, but she tried to go along with what Dustin wanted.

"The good wife," Julia mumbled as she chuckled under her breath. "That shit is for the birds."

But that's what she tried to be at first—t*he Good Wife.*

"More like a passive fucking idiot," she whispered.

Just the thought of Julia's previous attempt at staying married forever made her sick to her stomach. But after things blew up with her own family when she told them about her and Dustin's engagement to be married, what else could she do? She had to make it work. The disgusting names her mom and dad called Dustin *to his face* were something she'd been so ashamed of that she stopped speaking to her family for years.

But even though her family had been bigots towards her future husband, no one should be blocked entirely from their blood. Julia didn't expect Dustin to visit her family if he didn't want to, but there was no reason he should expect the same of her. Right? It was her mom and dad, for Christ's sake. They gave Julia her life. How could she stop talking to them forever?

But in time, it became evident that permanent separation is what Dustin expected of Julia. After four years of silence, Dustin didn't suggest making amends with her family. When Wilson and Michael were born, and Dustin still hadn't spoken about reaching out to her family, Julia took it upon herself to suggest it. One day at dinner, she asked Dustin if it would be okay to make a trip to let her family see the children. Dustin's over-the-top response by breaking all their dinnerware and flipping over their dining room table before calling up Grandma Noya and shitting on her family by calling them racists hurt Julia's soul. Dustin was perfectly content with his sons never seeing her family. But for Julia? She had to say yes to whatever her husband wanted: from hosting dinners with his boring ass clients to shunning all holidays even remotely associated with any injustice to his people.

"I was so fucking lame. Serves me right," whispered Julia. It wasn't long before Dustin viewed her desire to be a good wife as a license to allow him and his family to do whatever they wanted: The condescending way Dustin's mother spoke of her; the coded language; the soft-peddled demands; the smug way Dustin allowed Grandma Noya to insert her beliefs into their children and the overtly dismissive way Julia's beliefs got brushed aside whenever she opened her mouth about what she wanted for their sons.

"One thing is for sure. I'm not going to play the dumb fucking wife anymore!" she snapped as she stood on her tiptoes to see if Dustin was out of sight. Satisfied that he was gone, Julia stormed into the house, walked into the bedroom, and stared at the bed. She remembered what the ghost child had told her.

"Look under the bed. The book is there," Julia repeated. Slowly, she pulled the bed away from the wall. There was nothing there. Julia pulled the bed more until it was in the center of the room. The only thing she saw was a dusty hardwood floor.

"Fuck! Where is it?" she asked. Julia got down on her knees.

"Maybe it's caught on something," she said as she looked underneath. There was nothing. Frustrated, Julia stood up and was about to leave when two pale veined arms suddenly reached from under the bed and grabbed her ankles.

"AHHHHH!" Julia screamed.

Julia fell on her back, banging her head on the floor. The arms yanked at her ankle. *Hard.* Before she had time to react to the pain, the arms pulled her under the bed, and she was gone.

8

A Place Everyone Goes

"Are you going to lay there all night, or are you going to get up?"

Julia opened her eyes to see a huge shirtless Black man standing over her. Nervously, she sat up and looked around. A large campfire with blue flames flickered next to her legs. Julia didn't know why but she felt a huge desire to touch the fire. As if she couldn't control herself, she stuck out her hand to feel the warmth of the fire. Julia was surprised when a cold sensation crawled from her fingertips and up her arm. Soon her whole body became cold and numb. She quickly yanked her hand away and shoved her icy fingers into her mouth. After the coldness in her arm subsided, she turned to the man.

"Where am I? Who are you?" she asked.

The large man smiled and smacked his humongous belly.

"Look around. Be comfortable. Feel free to ask me whatever you like, but there's no guarantee I'll give you an answer. I'm a little fickle like that."

"Who are you? Where am I?" Julia repeated. Once again, the man ignored her questions.

"Get all the silly questions out of your system before we go to see Imani. She has the best food, and I don't want to be interrupted once the feast begins."

"Imani?"

"You requested her, didn't you?"

"No. I was just looking for a book."

"Ah, the book. I told Femi that would be confusing, but did he listen? That pain in the ass doesn't think sometimes. No wonder he crossed over so young. Please excuse me, sister. You were looking for answers?"

"Well...yeah."

"Imani has those for you."

Julia stood and looked around. She was in the middle of a dark field with dozens of campfires burning all around. She could see people of all races huddled over various colored campfires, none of them acknowledging the presence of the others while talking in a strange, whispered language.

"The fires you see are the places where the spirits of the living go to get their questions answered. I guess you would call those places dreams, but we call them Shulas."

"Um.... okay."

The man yawned and let out a thunderous burp. After rubbing his belly once more, he turned to Julia.

"You ready to go?"

Julia looked confused.

"Ready to go?" Julia asked. "Go where?"

"Imani's arriving soon. I have to take you to meet her."

The man extended his large hand to Julia.

"By the way, I'm Hakim."

Julia shook the man's hand. It was as hot as a stove. She instantly jerked her hand away and began blowing it. She quickly looked at her palm to see if it blistered. Her hand was normal.

"What the...."

Hakim cut her off before she could finish her sentence.

"You're Julia. We've been expecting you. Look, we don't have a lot of time to shoot the shit, okay? Shall we get going?"

Julia nodded. Hakim walked behind a large bush and grabbed a plastic container filled with orange liquid. He held it up to inspect the contents. After swishing it around a few times, Hakim unscrewed the container, sniffed it, and without warning turned to Julia and threw the container of fluid into her face.

"AAAAAHHH!" Julia screamed. Frantically she wiped at her face and coughed uncontrollably.

Hakim chuckled.

"I know. First time's a bitch, ain't it?"

"Are you some kind of maniac or something? What the hell did you do that for?" she yelled. The liquid smelled strange like maybe it was combustible. Terrified, Julia moved away from the blue flames. She began to think that perhaps the man was out to kill her.

"What did you throw on me?" Julia asked as she tried to squeeze the liquid out of her hair, looking at Hakim suspiciously.

"Relax, Julia. It's part of the process."

Julia smelled her hands.

"Process? What process? And what the hell is that smell? Is it gasoline? Kerosine? What did you throw on me?"

"That? Oh, that's squirrel piss and sugar."

"What?!"

Hakim burst out laughing.

"It's not really squirrel piss. It's transport fluid. But when you go home, you might encounter the smell one day. That's the best way to describe it. Squirrel piss and sugar."

Hakim raised the bucket high above his head and dumped the remaining liquid on himself. When all the fluid was gone, he lifted the container to his eye and looked inside.

"You ever been constipated?" he asked matter-of-factly. Julia was furious.

"What?!" she asked. "Get this shit off of me!"

Hakim continued talking as if Julia never responded.

"Constipation happens to everyone, right? But have you ever been so plugged that you could barely breathe? I mean, *really* backed up? I have. One time I couldn't take a shit for 40 years straight. That was one of the most painful things I've ever felt."

Julia's frustration boiled over.

"You're dead, aren't you, prick?"

Hakim pointed his fat finger at Julia and snickered.

"That's good. That's very good. But there are things you don't know about death until you die."

Julia continued wiping at her clothes.

"Oh yeah? Humor me. Like what?"

"Like pain. It continues."

"It does?"

"Hell yeah, it does. And it makes sense if you think about it. Most people believe life continues after death, so why wouldn't pain?"

"Because of heaven."

"You would think that, wouldn't you? But even in most of the religious text, there are hints at the continuance of pain. I mean, if there's a hell, why wouldn't there be pain?"

"You don't know if there's a heaven or hell?"

"Maybe Imani knows. As for me? I'm not that curious. Imani says I'm lazy. Maybe I am. All I know is that I was so constipated that I wanted to die. I mean, I'm already dead, but I wanted the pain to be gone. Do you know what I mean? Imagine eating every day with no relief. But one day, I drank transport fluid and poof! Problem solved. I shit so much that I lost 200 pounds in one week. Can you believe that?"

The man stuck his chubby finger inside the container before shoving it into his mouth. Julia stared at him in disbelief as he tongued the plastic container to find more liquid. Satisfied that none remained, he turned back to Julia.

"The first time's a bitch. I know. But trust me, it'll be over soon. You won't even remember this."

After tossing aside the container, he reached into the fire and grabbed a piece of burning wood. Instantly his whole body became engulfed in blue flame. Unable to see Hakim's face anymore, Julia turned to run. As soon as she took one step, Hakim tossed the burning log in her direction. She didn't get a chance to scream. Julia saw a blue flame envelope her vision, and then everything went black.

9 |

Something's Coming

"Hello, Princess," a soft milky voice spoke.

Julia opened her eyes and looked around. She was standing all alone on a beach with warm ocean water lapping gently at her feet.

"Where am I?" she asked.

"Where you need to be," the voice responded. Julia searched the beach, looking for the owner of the whisper. After realizing that she was the only person there, she rubbed her eyes and looked up into the night sky.

"Oh my God," she exclaimed.

The moon was so large that Julia lost her breath. All the rocks and craters on its surface were as clear as if she were there. The moondust sparkled like thousands of diamonds, each stone shimmering as it reflected the light of space.

"No way," Julia whispered.

Julia closed her eyes and opened her arms to take in as much of the celestial glow as possible. She took a step back and was shocked to see the moon draw closer to her, bathing her in golden moonlight. Soon she felt a sensation on her skin. The moonlight both warmed her face and cooled it at the same time. The light made her feel young and vibrant.

"It's beautiful, isn't it?" asked a voice. The voice seemed to be coming from across the water. Julia lowered her arms and looked out past the dark waves of the sea. Soon she saw the silhouette of a woman disappearing and reappearing like a figure distorted in the heat waves of the sun.

"I am Imani,"

"Where's Hakim?"

There was no answer. Suddenly the walking silhouette disappeared. Julia walked out a little further into the water but could not see anything. She cupped her hands around her mouth.

"Where are you?" she yelled.

"Beside you," the voice responded.

Julia turned and almost fell. An elderly *white* woman with long silver hair was standing beside her.

"Wait. You're white," a puzzled Julia exclaimed.

"Am I? I didn't realize," replied the woman in a slightly sarcastic tone.

A warm breeze blew and whipped the woman's hair into a mess, temporarily hiding her face. When her hair fell, Julia was standing before a tall Cherokee woman.

"Things are always confusing for the living," the woman said softly. "The colors you see are for your benefit, not mine. In this realm, segmenting souls based on skin color is a futile effort, wouldn't you agree?"

Julia said nothing. Instead, she raised her hands again and took in more moonlight.

Amused, the lady smiled and waited a few seconds before continuing.

"What is it that you want to know?"

"Everything."

"Be more specific."

Julia paused. She hadn't expected to get the answers to all her questions so directly. After thinking for a few moments, she responded.

"I don't know what to ask you."

Imani knelt, scooped up a handful of water, and splashed it on her face. When she lowered her hands, she was a young, thin African woman wearing a multicolored dress and matching headwrap.

"Start with your fear."

Julia looked over her shoulder. A dark menacing forest was on the edge of the beach. She could see hundreds of shadows inside, all swaying from left to right while fireflies lit and disappeared amongst them. Julia took a deep breath and spoke.

"My sons. Are they alive? Are they safe?"

"I can only speak of things that have happened. If you seek an omnipotent being, you have entered the wrong plane."

Julia thought for a moment. After formulating her line of questioning, she spoke.

"Have my sons died?"

"They have not."

Julia felt a wave of relief wash over her. She'd been so worried about her sons that she could hardly think of anything else. After a few seconds, a new question presented itself.

"The slaves."

Imani removed her headwrap, sat down in the water, and dipped her long black hair in the foam. Suddenly the water around her hair began bubbling, and dozens of giant crabs appeared. Several of them stuck out their claws and locked onto Imani's hair. Calmly she stood, shook a few of the crabs loose, and used one of the creatures as a comb to squeeze the excess water out of her hair. When she finished, Imani kissed the creature and lowered it into the next wave of water.

"Around here, we prefer to speak of them as spirits. They are no more slaves than you are dead."

"I'm not dead?"

"You are not dead."

"And you? Are you and Hakim dead?"

"The word *dead* makes things easy for the lazy to understand. Nothing dies. We transition."

Julia thought for a moment. It wasn't long before she felt embarrassed. Julia shouldn't have used the word slave to describe the spirits protecting her family. Sensing that she'd made a mistake, she quickly offered an apology.

"I'm sorry. I didn't mean to offend you by using that horrible word."
Imani smiled and reached out to touch Julia's hair.

"Such beautiful hair," she whispered. "I'm not offended, child. The spirits you see are just as much your brothers and sisters as they are mine. Redirect your apologies to them."

Julia smiled and stared at Imani's hair. It was the most beautiful hair Julia had ever seen. Just as she had felt at the campfire, Julia felt an uncontrollable urge. Slowly she reached out and grabbed a few strands of Imani's hair. Her eyes widened in surprise when the black strands changed to rainbow colors within her fingertips. Soon a warm sensation spread out from her fingers and traveled to Julia's chest. A soft vibrating sound started purring in her ears as a warm feeling engulfed her entire body.

"Ooooh...." Julia whispered, unable to control her blissful smile. Imani removed Julia's hand from her hair, kissed her palm, and let her hand fall gently by her side. Soon her smile disappeared, and a more solemn look appeared on her face.

"Tell me what you want to know, child."

"Well...about the spirits. Did my husband betray our family?"

"Ahhh. Loyalty or betrayal - a question most people would like answered about their spouses."

"Well?"

"The story Dustin told you is incomplete, and he's omitted several facts."

"Is the story he told me about the spirits true?"

"It is not."

"Will you tell me the truth?"

Imani wrapped her arms around Julia and gave her a tight hug. When she let go and stepped back, Imani was a little girl from India wearing a dark green dress made of silk and a red dot on her forehead.

"The truth begins with what you would call death."

Julia shook her head in acknowledgment.

"I know. Those people died because of slavery. Racism is so horrible."

"Is that what you think initiated their transition? Racism?"

"Well...yeah. That's how those spirits came to be, right?"

"From an abstract point of view, racism played a part. There's no doubt about it. But racism had very little to do with the termination of earthly life you see on that land."

"Really? How did they die?"

"Have you seen the spirit of Paul?"

"Paul?"

"He's an elderly spirit that roams around the property."

"Oh. Do you mean Dustin's Grandfather? Yes, I've seen him."

"Paul is primarily responsible for taking the earthly lives of the souls you see on that land."

Julia was surprised.

"What? What do you mean?"

"Paul and his wife killed them."

Julia thought about the little boy that instructed her to look under the bed. Next, she remembered the tiny girl that smiled at her just before entering the house. She felt a deep sadness for the children.

"Are you sure? How could this be?"

"Have you heard the stories about the forest in which the Tempest resides?"

"The Tempest?"

"Everything began there. In the beginning, the forest was vibrant and full of life. But eventually, things began to change. A fisherman complained of a creek running red with blood. Sometimes people complained of hearing screams of pain echoing through the forest late at night. Hunters began finding pieces of discarded machinery with chunks of human flesh stuck in their gears. It wasn't long before all wildlife began avoiding the area. Convinced that the area was cursed, the sharecroppers followed suit and forbade anyone from entering that forest. But Paul didn't listen to them. There was a certain curiosity that propelled him. Instead of steering clear of the evil in the woods, Paul ventured in to satisfy his curiosity. It wasn't long before the two found one another."

"You mean the man that took my son Michael? Mr. Green? Is that who you're talking about?"

"Yes. Mr. Green is the Tempest."

"Son of a bitch!" exclaimed Julia. She saw the ending of the story before Imani told her. Mr. Green had captured Dustin's great grandfather and tortured him. To get his freedom, Paul promised Mr. Green fresh souls.

Imani saw the look on Julia's face and smiled.

"Ahhhhh... I see that you're a quick study. Paul's first victim was a young Cherokee child named Kamama. Paul knew that her family allowed her to sometimes explore the creek on the edge of the forest. He captured her and gave her to Mr. Green to ratify their contract with one another – to provide the Tempest with an abundance of souls so that Paul could save his own."

Julia was furious. She knew the story Dustin told her didn't make sense, but she hadn't prepared herself for the amount of evil her husband was hiding.

"So, Paul is evil?"

"I can't answer that. The only thing I can tell you is what Paul is responsible for."

Julia bent down and splashed water on her face. When she stood again, Imani was a soldier with amputated legs sitting in a wheelchair. Julia was confused.

"Why did you take this appearance?" she asked, unhappy with what she was seeing. People with amputations scared her. They reminded her of the day her father lost his legs in a car accident.

"What do you mean?"

Julia looked away from the man.

"You're fucking with me," she snapped angrily. The man smiled and shook his head.

"Child, haven't you learned anything yet? I didn't take this appearance. You chose it for me."

Julia reached down and splashed more water on her face. When she looked at Imani again, she saw an enormous golden retriever with long blonde hair. The animal looked just like Julia's dog when she was a little girl.

"Mikey?" Julia asked as she held her open palm under the dog's nose. "It's me. Julia. Remember me?"

The dog stared straight ahead.

Finally, Julia heard Imani's voice echoing in her head.

"Paul bought his freedom by promising Mr. Green souls."

After realizing the dog standing before her was not her childhood pet, Julia lowered her hand and spoke.

"Why couldn't he accept death?"

"Fear, I suppose. Everyone is brave until faced with transitioning."

"So, he gave the souls of his community to Mr. Green?"

"Not quite. Paul gave up everyone *except* his community. He was afraid the people he lived and worked with would discover his evil deal. So instead of giving up the people he lived with, he traveled into town and convinced people he disliked most to go into the forest with him. Paul lured hundreds of them into the forest, and the Tempest accepted their souls as payment."

"So, if Paul didn't give his community to Mr. Green, what happened to them?"

"Soon, people in town began growing suspicious. Several important people disappeared, and rumors began circulating that Paul had seen the victims. Paul became afraid and stopped delivering souls to The Tempest."

"So, Mr. Green *did* kill them."

"No. The original deal was for the community's souls – the souls of the sharecroppers. But Paul never had the intention of turning them over to the Tempest. Somehow, he thought he would get himself out of the contract. But as time went on, it became apparent he could do nothing to free himself. When Paul stopped delivering the townspeople, the Tempest started looking for another victim to entrap. Eventually, a female sharecropper named Bess became that victim. Bess agreed to provide souls to save her life and promptly began delivering those souls to the Tempest in the forest. After four workers disappeared, Paul followed Bess into the forest and discovered her secret. Unsure of how to proceed, Paul went home and told his wife what he'd witnessed."

"Dustin's grandmother. I forgot her name. What was it?"

"Ama."

"That's it. Ama. She died recently."

Imani cracked a slight smile that puzzled Julia. Trying her best to ignore what she saw, Julia let Imani continue with her story.

"Although Ama was a simple woman, she had a wrinkle in her soul that wasn't visible to most people – including her husband. Paul expected his wife to leave him. After telling Ama of his deal with the Tempest, there would be no way his nice, quiet wife would be able to tolerate or even comprehend the evil behavior he'd demonstrated. Still, Paul had nowhere to turn. It would only be a matter of time before the Tempest pushed Bessie to arrive at his home to kill the both of them. Paul had to tell his wife everything that night, and he did, not only out of a need for guidance but also their survival."

"What happened?"

"Their bond became unbreakable. For them, their bond was eternally sealed. For the sharecroppers? That night was their destruction. Some loves should never exist, but sometimes do."

"Isn't that the truth."

Julia thought of her failed marriage and all the problems she and Dustin had. If only she had left Dustin before having his kids, maybe they both would be happier.

"That night, Ama indeed became Paul's eternal partner. Together they devised a plan to deny the Tempest his bounty of souls. First, they kidnapped Bess and took her into the cornfields. Once there, they killed her and buried her body. Next, they crept into the community and took the earthly lives of the remaining sharecroppers as they slept in their beds. With the final worker dead, Paul returned to his home with his wife. After taking a bath and enjoying a nice meal, he kissed Ama goodbye and gave her a final gift."

"What was it?"

"He gave Ama his sugar cane machete and allowed her to cut his head off. She buried it beneath the floorboards of their home."

Julia shivered and wrapped her arms around her shoulders.

"Gruesome!"

Imani shrugged.

"Visually, maybe. But a pointless act. Once the soul leaves, there is only a shell."

Julia thought about the story Imani had just told her.

"Their home....their home," she repeated. "Where is the house located?"

"You're currently residing in it," replied Imani.

Julia felt sick to her stomach.

"And Paul's head?"

"Under the floorboards in the bedroom."

Julia leaned over and gagged as the need to vomit overcame her.

"I think I'm going to be sick."

The dog looked at Julia for a few moments and then licked itself. Julia felt sick. She'd made love to Dustin in that bedroom. Now she understood why she'd seen the ghost of Dustin's grandfather. His head was in there!

After gaining control, Julia stood again.

"Relax, child. The only thing remaining under that floorboard is a skull. You're perfectly safe."

"Safe?! My sons are gone, and I'm sleeping with my husband in a goddamned cemetery!"

"It could be worse. You could be one of the spirits."

Julia considered the story of Dustin's grandfather and lowered her voice before speaking.

"What a pair of selfish jerks! Paul could've just sacrificed himself. Instead, he kills everyone?"

"I guess Paul thought he and his wife would be saving the souls of everyone in the community. And for a while, it worked. That is until the Tempest discovered the truth. What you are seeing now is anger at that agreement being unfulfilled."

"Wait. If Paul killed those people, how can he stay on that land with them? Wouldn't they be angry? Why are they protecting Paul and his family from Mr. Green? Why aren't they here?"

"Noya."

Julia felt a jolt of anger at the mention of the woman's name.

"Ama's daughter?"

"That is the one."

"How is she mixed up in all this? The killings happened before she was born, right?"

"Noya was a baby when this happened. Ama and Paul agreed that they should spare her life to continue their bloodline."

"Selfish idiots! How was Ama able to avoid Mr. Green for so long? Didn't he go searching for her?"

"Ama and Noya are not who you think they were. They are clair-voyants."

"Witches?"

"If that name helps you, fine. But it would be more beneficial to you if you thought of the tools they use as Dark Power. It exists on different levels, and its use is not forbidden."

"Wait, you allow the use of black magic? You allow witches to exist?"

"Certainly. As long as no one is hurt to gain access, the Creator doesn't mind. He views it no different than wealth. Some people will have it, and some people won't. It's what that person does with wealth when it's in their possession that will determine judgment. And so it is with Dark Power."

Julia shook her head.

"This is weird."

"Now we disagree with how Noya and Ama are currently using Dark Power. They played with Dark Power until they found a way to avoid detection. They do it by using the souls of the people they murdered to protect themselves. That is a certified violation of the highest priority that brings immediate judgment."

Julia was flabbergasted.

"That's.... that's disgusting! Isn't that...."

"Slavery. Yes, it is. But it's far worse. Ama took the lives of the sharecroppers, and now she's turned their souls into her slaves using powers from a dark plane of existence. It's complete and total ownership. Ama told her family that she only used the spell to hide them, that they were only using them for protection from the Tempest and his army. But her true intention is much more sinister. She intends to use the sharecroppers as the foundation to build her army of soldiers. Ama wants to build an army of undead to take over the world. She's jealous of Mr. Green and wants to eliminate him. Ama and Mr.Green's goals are the same."

"How can you allow Ama and Noya to do this? Shouldn't you be trying to stop them immediately? How can you allow Mr. Green to go around killing people?"

"The decision is not ours to make. This place is just a depot of souls – a place where there is an accounting of arrivals. Everyone goes to other planes of existence, and some stay here with us. Others go to the reincarnation fields, and some go to the great sleep. But for exceptional violations that interrupt the flow of lifeforce, judgment is immediate when God decides. For us, we must allow all their decisions to be counted and recorded."

"So Noya and her mom are going to be judged?"

"Once the mother and daughter found the Dark Power, they used it to avoid detection and kept the souls of the sharecroppers on the plane of the living. But in doing this, they also denied God's realm of receiving those souls. Ama and Noya kept the spirits blind to the truth. God isn't ignoring their violations. He's just waiting patiently for the recording of their sins. When their life-forces finally pass, his judgment will be mighty."

Julia's eyes widened as the next question entered her head.

"Are Noya and her mother dead?"

"No one is dead."

"Don't play coy with me. I'm not in the mood."

"Their souls have not crossed over."

"Is my husband aware of this?"

"He was there when Noya and Ama made their plans, and he has been a part of their plan from the beginning."

"Where are they?"

"Once again, I can't tell you of their current predicament. I can only reveal what has happened."

Julia stopped talking and closed her eyes. Suddenly her eyes popped open.

"The water well behind the house!"

Imani remained silent.

"Why did they involve my sons?"

"They used the Dark Power on your oldest."

"Wilson. Yeah, I know. His eye. That came from them? But why?"

"They're using him."

"For what?"

Imani remained silent.

"Come on! Tell me, damn it!"

The dog began growling and circling in front of Julia.

"Please remember yourself. Confrontation is not something taken lightly on this plane," whispered Imani. Julia noticed the growling dog and lowered her voice.

"I'm sorry. I'm not mad at you. It's just, how dare Noya and her family use my sons! How could they be so cruel?"

Finally, the dog stopped growling. Julia wiped the tears from her eyes and began looking around.

"I've got to go. How do I get out of here?"

"The same way you entered."

"Where's Hakim? He's the way out of here, right?"

"He is."

Julia heard footsteps approaching from behind. She turned to see Hakim walking out of the forest chewing on a gigantic leg of meat.

"Hey, Imani! This roasted chicken is awesome! You got any more?"

The dog began barking excitedly and running in circles, trying to reply to the man's question. Hakim laughed and took another bite from the chicken leg.

"I know. I know. I'll go on a special diet for you, okay? But not today."

Hakim walked up to Julia and stopped. Julia took one whiff of what the man was eating and gagged.

"That's chicken?" she asked as she held her nose and backed away. The golden retriever looked at Hakim from head to toe and slowly backed away.

"That's not the chicken I prepared," said Imani. Hakim burst into laughter once more.

"I added a few special ingredients. Eagle droppings, earthworms, and skunk juice. It's better this way."

Hakim held the meat out underneath Julia's nose.

"Here. Try it."

Julia gagged once more.

"I've got to get out of here. How do I go home?" asked Julia.

"Hakim, that's disgusting," said Imani.

"Whatever. You two don't know good food," Hakim replied as he devoured the remaining meat on the bone. Once the bone was clean, he threw it into the ocean and turned to Imani.

"Did you tell her?" he asked.

"Not yet," replied the voice Julia had first heard when Imani arrived. Julia turned and saw the African girl standing before her once more.

"Tell me what? I have to go. Now!"

"Remember when I told you we couldn't see the future?"

"Yes."

"There is an exception. In instances of enormous transfers of energy between planes, we are allowed to see how those transfers originate."

"You mean life and death?"

"Yes."

"Look, I really need to be getting back."

"Look into the forest."

Julia turned and looked into the dark forest. She saw the same shadowy figures that she'd seen earlier.

"Those shadows are spirits of the dead that are soon to come."

"Yeah? And? Please, I need to get home."

Imani raised her right arm into the air.

"Prepare yourself."

A giant bolt of lightning struck Imani's raised arm, and everything went black. Suddenly a finger snapped, and light returned. Julia stared in awe.

"What the...."

The group was standing on the black waters of the ocean with millions of shadows around them.

"All of the shadows you see are of people that will transition."

"All of these people will die?"

"Yes. We don't know how or why, but we do know that death is approaching."

Hakim moved closer to Julia. Although she could still smell the rank odor of his dinner, the power of what she was witnessing was greater.

"Wilson," said Hakim.

The sound of the man saying her son's name snapped Julia out of her trance.

"Wilson? What about my son?"

"Your son is at the center of it all."

Julia turned to Imani.

"The center of it all? What does he mean? Are you saying that my son is going to kill all these people?"

"At this moment, we can only see his involvement."

Julia stared into the millions of shadows.

"I don't understand. I mean, you're mistaken. Wilson can't be...."

"There are only two things certain about the outcome - the scale of the loss of life and Wilson's involvement."

"Is it Mr. Green?"

"No."

"No? What do you mean, no? Who else is running around killing and torturing people?"

"The Tempest does possess the power to murder on this magnitude, but your son's power is greater than his. Wilson just hasn't realized it yet."

"Greater?"

"Noya and Ama gave your son the power through supernatural methods. Based on what we know of the sources they accessed, your son's power is greater than any person we've seen in 200 years."

"So, you think my son could be this mass murderer?"

"The possibility exists because Ama created it. We just don't know if he's the source of all the death yet."

Julia turned to Hakim.

"I want to go home. Now."

Hakim held up his hands in protest.

"Okay, but..."

Imani stepped in front of Hakim and grabbed Julia by both arms.

"I understand you want to confront Noya and Ama for what they've done to your son, but you don't have the weapons or the skill to engage them directly."

Julia tried pushing Imani out of the way but could not move her. Frustrated, she began crying.

"Send me home now! I've got to stop them! They can't get away with this. Those are my children!"

Julia lowered her head into her hands and began sobbing while Imani gently began rubbing her arm.

"I was also a vessel for a soul," Imani whispered. "Actually, my earth husband and I helped four souls begin their travels."

Julia lifted her head.

"You mean pregnancy? You had four children?"

"Yes. So, I understand your desire to intervene in defense of those souls. The love of a mother is one of the most powerful things in the universe."

"Then why are you trying to stop me?"

"Because you do not have the proper weapons to go against Noya and Ama."

Julia's eyes widened, and she wiped the tears from her face.

"I don't have the proper weapons, but you do!"

Imani shook her head.

"We cannot get involved. It is forbidden."

"Forbidden? You brought me here and gave me this information. You're already involved."

Imani turned to Hakim, and he shook his head.

"We cannot get involved in the physical sense," said Imani.

"But isn't bringing me here the *physical* sense?" Julia asked angrily.

"It's not the same," whispered Hakim.

Julia stomped her feet and clenched her fists.

"Please! My son needs your...."

Imani held up her palm and interrupted Julia before she could finish.

"We cannot get involved. It is forbidden."

Julia angrily turned to Hakim.

"Take me home."

Imani extended her arm to the sky, and lightning struck it again. Within seconds they were back on the beach. Julia immediately turned away from Imani and began walking.

"Which way are we supposed to go?" Julia asked. Hakim looked at Imani briefly before following Julia.

"It's this way. Follow me."

As they continued walking on the cool sand, Julia looked back to see that Imani had disappeared.

"Thanks for nothing," she whispered.

Julia and Hakim continued walking on the beach for half a mile before a large bonfire rose out of the darkness.

"She's right, you know."

"Who? Imani?"

"We could get into a lot of trouble by not following the rules."

"Look, Imani already said no to helping me. It's okay. I get it."

Suddenly Hakim stopped.

"*We* can't get involved, but *I* can."

Julia's eyes filled with joy.

"Could you? It would mean the world to me if you could...."

"Shut up."

Hakim stared at Julia for a few moments before continuing.

"Ama and Noya are going to stop you from leaving that house. But there's a way for you to escape."

Hakim looked around to make sure no one was watching.

"I could get into a lot of trouble for telling you this, but these deaths are an enormous problem. Everyone's afraid—even Imani. And no one is speaking about how bad it's going to be. But I know. I had a dream."

"How bad will it be?"

"Let's just say that it's going to be worse than Imani showed you."

"How?"

"In two nights, there will be a lunar eclipse - Oshua's Red Moon."

"Oshua's Red Moon. What is that?"

"Just a fancy way of saying the moon will...."

Hakim gave Julia an annoyed look and sucked his teeth in frustration.

"Look, lazy ass, I don't have time to explain shit for you. I thought you were smart, but maybe you're dumb as a fucking rock for all I know. Take a science class."

Julia smirked at Hakim's weak insult. It was kind of funny coming from a man with a body shaped like an enormous tea kettle. Still, she took heed to what he said and kept her opinions to herself.

"Is that all you can tell me?"

"The most important thing to know is that a mystical event will happen within the eclipse that permanently changes life as you know it. None of us knows what it is, which means it's probably stronger than anything in our realm. All we know is that a massive amount of death will sweep the earth for years because of it."

"Okay. No worries. But very little surprises me at this point. I don't know how to break the news to you, but I'm living in a graveyard. It doesn't get worse than that."

"It can get worse, and it will. You wait and see. Everything's going to get much worse."

"When will those bitches try to stop me from leaving?"

"The forest is too dangerous for you right now. Your best bet is to wait until Oshua's Red Moon. It's the only time Mr. Green's minions will be too distracted to attack you. Now, I've said all that I can say."

"But...."

Hakim's eyes got wide, and suddenly, he screamed out at Julia.

"Get out of here!"

Hakim ran into the center of the bonfire. He grabbed two large burning logs from the center of the fire and sprinted out, his legs still aflame. He winced slightly as the fire burned his body from the waist down. Julia recoiled in fear as a large grin spread across Hakim's face.

"Don't worry. The trip back isn't as bad as the arrival," Hakim's deep voice boomed.

Hakim smashed both burning logs into Julia's head, making her eyeballs shoot out of her skull. Julia seemed unaware of what happened and opened her mouth to speak, blood oozing from her eye sockets.

"You're right. This trip isn't so bad—everything's dark. I want to go to sleep," Julia whispered in a gargled voice.

Suddenly her whole body burst into purple flame, and a strong breeze began blowing across the beach.

"Good trip, pretty lady," whispered Hakim as he watched the ashes of Julia's body blow away into the night breeze. After Julia had disappeared, Hakim turned to face the fire once more. He rubbed his ample belly and released a large burp into the night air. Suddenly Hakim got a running start and dove headfirst into the large fire.

"Remember not to go into the forest before the eclipse! It's your only hope of escaping!" he screamed as he laughed uncontrollably in the fire. As the flames crawled up his torso and enveloped his face, Hakim continued laughing joyfully. Soon his laughter stopped as the fire melted the skin from his skull. Seconds later, a massive wave rose from the dark waters and crashed into the beach, extinguishing the bonfire and pulling all evidence of any visitors into the sea.

10

Open the Gates

"I've seen this place before," whispered Wilson. "We're at the entrance."

The three boys crouched down behind the rubble that used to be Wilson's great-grandmother's house and stared at the forest of flashing lights.

"Oh yeah? How do you know this is the entrance?" asked Tariq.

"Grandma Noya showed it to me," replied Wilson.

He remembered the day he and Michael spent the night with Grandmother Noya. The memory was so fresh in his mind that it seemed like it happened yesterday. Wilson remembered how Grandma Noya had pulled back the curtains to let him see the evil world that remained invisible to others. She explained to him how their family had been responsible for protecting the world from hell's invasion and how one day he'd be required to assume that duty.

Wilson missed Grandma Noya. She didn't just explain things to him; she *showed* him. Because of her, Wilson learned of the incredible power he had. Grandma Noya taught him to see creatures that would terrify an average child. She didn't mince words with Wilson. His age was irrelevant. Although he was a child, his grandmother gave him the truth, and he respected her for it.

Along with revealing his gift, Grandma Noya taught Wilson to suppress his fear. She schooled him not to let his emotions get the best of him. If not for her teachings, Wilson would never have had the courage to try to rescue his little brother from the jaws of hell. And there would be no way he would have the courage to fight back against Mr. Green. Grandma Noya gave Wilson the information along with enough skill to fight back against the evil - the nightmare that sat on the edge of his Great Grandmother's yard.

"How are we supposed to go in unnoticed with all that activity?" asked Tariq.

"Not to mention the fact that we don't even know where Michael is," chimed in Takatoka.

"I'm sure there's a way. We'll find Michael. I can feel it," Wilson lied. But inside, he knew Takatoka was right. They were on a mission to save his little brother without knowing where he might be or how to get to him.

As the boys watched the forest light up in strange colors they'd never seen before, Wilson searched his memory for anything that could give him a clue to Michael's whereabouts. Meticulously, he ran over the day of his brother's kidnapping:

His brother had been unconscious as the worms burst from his chest and dragged him to the forest. Their parents ran out of the house to pursue their son much too late to do or say anything. The ghostly spirits that witnessed the event didn't speak about the kidnapping. Aside from the ghost of the little girl who shrieked to alert Wilson's family, none of the spirits uttered a word.

And then there was Mr. Green, the man who had kidnapped Michael. Other than the thick veins that appeared in Wilson's face whenever he was close by, Wilson could glean nothing from his interactions with the man. He had never heard the man utter a single word. He'd only seen the man once, yet Wilson feared him beyond comprehension. Mr. Green didn't look like the other spirits that Wilson saw. Something terrified him about his physical presence; the air around Mr. Green seemed murky, like the fumes pouring out of the muffler of an old car. Mr. Green seemed to be there, but not entirely of their world.

His clothes stuck to him as though a part of his body. And then there was the smell of the man; even after he was long gone, the stink from Mr. Green remained hanging in the forest like the rank air of an old abandoned house.

After realizing that there were no clues in the past events, Wilson's mind once again drifted to his grandmother. Were there any clues she'd given him? Was he missing an important message? He racked his brain, trying to remember all the things she'd told him. But after several minutes, he gave up. There were no verbal breadcrumbs that would magically lead them to Michael's location in the forest. If they were going to find Michael, they would need to rely on their ability to fight – that plus a whole lot of luck.

"Look! The bushes are moving!" whispered Takatoka as he pointed towards the edge of the forest.

Suddenly an enormous wild boar emerged from the shadows. The pig had glowing red eyes and seemed to be a creature of hell's creation. It made strange sounds as it walked; it both grunted like a pig and growled like a rabid dog. Half the animal's face was missing; the cartilage, blood vessels, and teeth were all exposed. Giant yellow maggots ate at the open tissue on the boar's face causing the animal to shake its head every few steps, slinging thick foam from its mouth as it tried to get rid of the pests. As it did so, a smell finally reached the boys causing them to cover their mouths and noses in disgust.

"Dude! The smell!"

"It smells just like Calian did!"

"That's some seriously gross stuff!"

Suddenly the creature raised its massive head and released a blood-curdling scream so loud that it shook the ground.

"Holy shit!" Takatoka exclaimed, pointing towards the creature. Wilson immediately slapped his hand over his mouth.

"You've got to be quiet!" Wilson whispered. "That thing might hear us!"

After a few moments, Takatoka peeked around the corner of the debris.

"Shit!" he exclaimed.

"What is it?" asked Tariq.

"I think it has our scent," replied Takatoka.

Wilson took his turn and leaned out to look at the animal. The boar had its head lifted and sniffed as if it could smell something in the air. Wilson immediately ducked back into his hiding place.

"We've just got to find a way around it," Wilson replied as he tried unsuccessfully to hide his fear. Tariq saw the fear in Wilson's eyes and leaned out to take another look for himself. He immediately darted back into hiding.

"It has our scent for sure!"

Unable to contain their boyhood curiosity, all three boys simultaneously looked out from their hiding place. As if aware of their location, the animal turned to face them.

"Fuck. Fuck. Fuck," whispered Tariq.

Wilson bit down on his lip, leaned over, and prepared to take another look. Takatoka grabbed his arm and yanked him back.

"Dude! Are you crazy?! If that thing sees us, we're dead!"

"We've got to find a way in! We don't have a choice!"

It had been several days since Mr. Green took Wilson's brother and Wilson was determined to find a way to save Michael. Although he was terrified by the demonic creature that seemed to be standing guard in front of the forest, Wilson could hear Grandma Noya's words of encouragement pushing him to move forward. Time was running out to save his little brother, and they had to do something.

Wilson pushed away Takatoka's hand and leaned out to take another look. The boar's searing red eyes immediately locked on Wilson, and it took off in a wild sprint towards their hiding spot.

"Fucking idiot! See what you did?" whispered Takatoka.

Wilson prepared to touch his eyelid to access his powers.

"Hey, Takatoka. You and..."

Wilson turned to Takatoka, but the boy was gone. Wilson searched the ground until he saw several foot imprints moving away from their location in the early morning dew.

"I'll be over here in the bushes," whispered an invisible Takatoka.

Wilson turned to Tariq.

"Your power is communicating with animals, right?"

"What? Do you expect me to try to communicate with that thing? You've got to be kidding me! I communicate with regular animals - Bambi and shit like that. If I try to go inside that thing's mind, it might take control of me! No fucking way!"

Wilson checked to see how far the animal was from reaching them. Although the animal was running uphill toward their location, it was still moving fast. Wilson raised his finger to touch his eyelid. Just as he was about to activate his powers, the charging animal suddenly stopped. It lowered its head and released a scream that made the boys cover their ears.

"It's hurt," exclaimed Tariq. "Look!"

The animal cried out again and began flailing about uncontrollably.

"Why is it screaming?" asked Wilson. "I don't see anything."

"There!" exclaimed Tariq as he pointed towards the sky. Wilson looked up. A small black cloud suddenly appeared in the clear night sky. Slowly it began to grow larger.

"Is it that guy? Mr. Green?" asked Tariq.

Wilson remembered what happened to his face whenever Mr. Green was close. Slowly, he ran his fingers across his cheek. Feeling only his soft skin, Wilson breathed a sigh of relief. Had the evil man been present, his face would have been swollen and deformed with thick veins.

"No. I don't think it's Mr. Green. That cloud is something different."

As the cloud continued growing, the boar began leaping in a panic, bucking like a wild bronco, trying to evade the black cloud above it.

"Why is it jumping around like that?" asked Tariq.

"I don't know," replied Wilson.

There was a sizzling sound to Wilson's right. Both he and Tariq turned to see Takatoka reappear out of thin air. Takatoka quickly lowered himself to his knees beside the boys.

"What's going on?" he asked as they stared at the spectacle in front of the forest.

But Wilson and Tariq said nothing as they continued staring at the cloud. The boys watched in amazement as several bolts of lightning struck the ground around the boar, creating a circle of fire. The creature froze and lowered its head. Suddenly dozens of vultures with wings made of fire poured out of the cloud and descended on the area. They flew in a circular pattern in front of the forest like a vast burning blanket, screaming like banshees as if searching for prey. The pig could do nothing but tremble. The birds made several passes in front of the forest. Once they were satisfied there was no other prey, the birds flew high into the night sky and stayed afloat without moving. One by one, each of the birds swooped down from the sky and took their turn at ripping a chunk of flesh from the boar's back.

The boys gasped in horror at the brutality of it all. They had never seen such a heinous act carried out so deliberately. The boar looked evil, and its eyes seemed to burn with the same hellfire that fueled the birds' wings. And yet, the vultures took turns eating the animal, careful to inflict as much pain as possible. It was as though the animals were delivering a message to any creature watching.

Unable to escape its fate, the pig could do nothing but scream. Weak from the pain and no longer able to withstand the onslaught, the boar crashed to the ground in a large pool of blood, twitching as its glowing red eyes remained fixed on the boys. Finally, when the light of hell stopped glowing in the animal's eyes, the boys knew the animal was dead.

The hellish birds continued feasting on the pig's flesh until there was nothing but bones left. Still hungry, the birds cracked open the bones and began picking at the marrow.

"Maybe we should get out of here," whispered a nervous Takatoka. Wilson agreed. Still, he couldn't take his eyes off the demonic creatures feasting on one of their own. What they were seeing would be much worse if one of the creatures saw the boys. Still, Wilson was unable to move. Seeing such a thing was like seeing an approaching tornado, knowing he should run, but unable to take his eyes off of what he was seeing.

When the bones were empty, the birds began squawking angrily at one another. Eventually, they started fighting.

"Oh shit!" exclaimed Tariq.

One of the vultures ripped the head off another vulture and began pulling meat from its carcass. After seeing the bird with fresh meat in its mouth, another bird attacked, slicing at the creature until it stopped moving. Another vulture attacked that bird, ripped its wings off, and attempted to eat the injured bird whole.

This display of carnage went on for a few more moments when suddenly, the earth underneath the creatures began to move. Soon the ground collapsed, and a great scream rose as burning feathers scattered everywhere.

"What's that? What's happening?" asked Tariq.

"No fucking way!" whispered Wilson.

The three boys watched in horror as dozens of tiny *human* babies climbed out of the hole, each of them with deep cuts all over their bodies, shrieking like rabid animals. Some of them had decaying flesh that fell from their bones as they moved. Others had deep dents in their skulls as if something had fallen on their heads. But they all seemed insane with hunger. Thick, pink saliva dripped from the corners of their mouths as their eyes combed the ground, searching for anything to eat. One by one, their eyes fell on the mostly eaten carcasses of the vultures, and they attacked them, shoving them hungrily into their mouths. They screamed out in glee as they used their razor-sharp black teeth to bite into the birds. They bit and clawed at one another, attempting to eat their portion of the remaining scraps. When the birds were gone, the babies angrily banged their skulls against the earth and cried out in agony. After seeing a few drops of blood on the ground, some babies scooped up handfuls of dirt and shoved their hands into their open mouths. Tasting the blood on their fingers and forgetting who the blood-soaked fingers belonged to, each of them bit down hungrily and tried to eat their own hands.

Wilson looked over at Takatoka and Tariq, their faces as white as sheets. Wilson knew what was running through their minds. What they were watching wasn't like what they'd experienced in the forest during the beginning of their journey. That experience felt like a horror movie because death wasn't so evident. But this was different. Something was playing out before their very eyes that was much more sinister. Here, actual death was on display; creatures that only lived in nightmares took life and could take theirs.

"Come on," whispered Wilson. "Let's go."

"Where?" asked Tariq.

"This forest stretches for miles. We'll try to enter from another location."

Careful to remain hidden, Wilson turned on his knees and crawled away from the forest with Takatoka and Tariq following closely behind.

Suddenly something rang out from the forest that made the boys freeze in their tracks.

"We see you! You cannot escape us!"

Terrified, the boys looked at one another in disbelief.

"No way!"

"It can't be!"

One by one, they turned around and stared at the edge of the forest. Standing in front of it was a young boy that they recognized.

"It can't be. Is that Calian?" asked Takatoka.

"Yep. That's Calian, or at least what *used* to be him," replied Wilson.

"My God. They really fucked him up," replied Tariq.

Calian stood shirtless with a long broad suture stretching from his neck to groin. His eyes were gone, and two long rusty spikes were sticking out of his eye sockets. The gigantic arm the boys had seen on Calian was now a living horror; it was boneless, flipping uncontrollably like a snake with an enormous mouth full of teeth.

"Wilson. We know where Michael is," Calian said, his voice sounding demonic. "Don't you want our help?"

"Fuck you!" whispered Wilson under his breath.

"Michael begs us to come home. Don't you want his pain to end?" said Calian, smiling as he spoke of the boy.

"Fuck you!" Wilson said louder.

Tariq grabbed Wilson's wrist.

"Chill, bro. He's just trying to make you pissed," Tariq whispered.

A devious smile appeared on Calian's face that angered Wilson much more. The thought that this thing had his brother tied up somewhere made his blood boil. Any remorse he felt for Calian was gone, replaced by a hatred of the boy that grew by the second.

Suddenly Calian extended his serpent arm and grabbed one of the babies by its skull. A loud crunching noise sounded like someone walking on gravel rumbled through the air. Next came a long hollow slurping followed by gulping. Wilson felt sick to his stomach. They were listening to the sounds of Calian killing and drinking the insides of one of the babies. Within seconds the infant's body was nothing but a pile of purplish raisinlike skin on the ground. Black goo began pouring out of Calian's eye sockets as a long tongue extended from the boy's mouth. Hungrily Calian licked at his face until all the black liquid was gone.

"Sick fuck!" cursed Takatoka.

"I never liked that son of a bitch," added Tariq.

Wilson looked away from the monster, his mind going crazy as he imagined what might be happening to his little brother. Calian burst into a contemptuous laugh that made Wilson grit his teeth. The creature was reading his mind.

"Your brother's fate will soon be the same as yours!" yelled Calian.

The monster child extended his serpent arm in the direction of the boys.

"We want him!" commanded Calian. As if heeding the boy's command, thousands of eyes lit up the forest behind him. Suddenly all the trees of the forest started shaking violently. Calian's snake arm detached from his body and went slithering up the hill after the boys.

"Run!" yelled Wilson. But he didn't need to say anything to his two friends. As soon as Takatoka and Tariq saw the trees shaking, they all but sprinted away from the forest.

"Wilson! Let's go!" screamed Takatoka as he activated his power and melted away into the darkness.

"Come on!" yelled Tariq.

Calian yanked one of the rusty spikes from his eye socket and threw it high into the air. The piece of metal flew over the boys and landed in the soil in front of them. Suddenly the metal turned orange, igniting a large fire in front of the kids.

"You cannot escape us!" Calian's voice boomed.

Suddenly a loud screeching noise sounded, making the boys cover their ears. Wilson turned around and lost his breath at what he saw. There were thousands of babies climbing the hill in pursuit of the boys. Wilson turned to Tariq.

"Whatever power you have, you'd better use it now."

"I know. It's just that...."

"Do you see what's coming for us? Use it!"

"Okay. Remember, you asked for it. But once I use my powers, I can't use them again for 24 hours."

"Just use them already!"

Tariq squeezed his eyes shut and began chanting.

"Come the light! Come the light! Come the light!"

Tariq began sweating as though someone had poured a bucket of water on his head. A white fog enveloped the boy, and he started coughing. Soon he disappeared.

"Tariq! Where are you?" asked Wilson.

"I'm here!" responded Tariq.

Wilson saw a strange figure standing inside the fog and moved towards it. He jumped when he saw what stepped out of the smoke. Standing before Wilson was a creature that he'd never seen before.

"Tariq?" asked Wilson, unsure if the boy was inside the creature.

"Yeah, it's me," Tariq replied. "Don't look at me like that. I tried to tell you it would be different."

"I know, but...."

Different didn't explain what Wilson was seeing. Tariq looked like a walking science experiment. Although his arms and hands were human, nothing else was. Tariq had two eyes on either side of his face, with one gigantic eyeball sitting in the center of its forehead. Half his face was a lion's, while the other half was a bear's. His skin sparkled like diamonds and seemed to move every few seconds – like he had snakes all over his body. His legs were so muscular that they looked like he was walking on tree trunks. His toes, which had shredded his shoes, were made of gigantic multicolored beetles that hissed whenever he took a step. A thick coat of spiderwebs was on his back, with different colored arachnids crawling in and out of the strands.

Wilson looked at Tariq a few seconds more and then turned to the approaching army of demons. He touched his eye to activate his powers. Once again, the world that Wilson saw melted away, and a new world drenched in a reddish haze came into view. Unable to contain his curiosity about Tariq's actual appearance, Wilson looked at the "thing" that had once been his friend. What he saw was a large-mouthed Shih Tzu puppy cloaked in a ghostly spirit that changed randomly from a tiger to a gorilla to a dolphin and then a colorful Toucan bird.

"What do you want me to do?" asked Tariq's voice.

"Fight!" yelled Wilson.

Wilson turned to look down the hill. It was the first time he'd looked at the invading mob of babies since he used his powers. The babies chasing them were not babies at all – they were the souls of demons from hell.

Tariq opened his mouth, and several animal sounds escaped at once.

"What the hell was that?" asked Wilson after hearing the strange sounds coming from his friend's throat.

"I'm calling reinforcements," explained Tariq. Suddenly Takatoka reappeared beside his friends.

"They'd better come fast. We're out of time," yelled Takatoka before disappearing once more.

Wilson turned around in time to see several of the demonic creatures leap into the air. He concentrated on the babies, extended his arms out in front of him, and grabbed. In doing so, an invisible force held the monsters in the air. Before the demons could break free, Wilson squeezed his empty hands together and watched as the babies exploded, shooting black liquid all over Tariq.

"Damn, dude! Can't you be more careful?" asked Tariq, wiping black goo from his strange body.

"You want me to let that demon baby bite you?" snapped Wilson.

"Watch what you're doing next time. Fuck!" complained Tariq.

Suddenly a tiny bird landed on Wilson's shoulder. It tilted its head to stare at the boy quizzically before flying in the direction of the approaching monsters.

"They're here," exclaimed Tariq.

There was a ruffling above the boys, and suddenly the sky turned black. Thousands of birds flew over the boys' heads and began attacking the creatures at the bottom of the hill.

"Holy shit!" yelled Takatoka, materializing once more.

All three boys watched in surprise as the birds attacked relentlessly. The baby demons screamed out as the birds poked, ripped, and clawed at their faces, pushing the creatures back into the forest.

Tariq started coughing uncontrollably and fell to his knees. Wilson ran to his side.

"You okay?"

"No....I can't."

Suddenly Tariq's whole body burst into flame. Wilson backed away from the boy as he fell to the ground and began rolling around in pain.

"Stay away!" yelled Tariq.

Wilson and Takatoka backed away, unsure of how to proceed. Wilson looked at the bottom of the hill and saw what was happening. The birds that came to do battle with the demons were losing. Although they had managed to push the demonic babies back into the forest, Calian had begun spraying fire from his eye sockets, burning the birds as they flew overhead.

Wilson turned his attention back to Tariq; the fire was out, and his body returned to its original state, but he was naked with ice crystals all over his skin.

"Help me....find my clothes," Tariq whispered, shaking uncontrollably. Wilson and Takatoka looked around the area. They eventually found the rags that had once been Tariq's clothing.

"Come on, guys," whispered Wilson. "Let's get out of here while Calian's busy."

Suddenly Tariq began sobbing uncontrollably.

"He killed them! They were my friends!"

Takatoka looked at Wilson with a confused look on his face.

"What is he talking about?"

"The birds."

Tariq looked at the dozens of burning birds pouring from the sky with tears streaming down his face. Suddenly he became enraged. He looked down the hill at a gleeful Calian, streams of flames shooting from his eye sockets, burning as many birds as he could.

"I'm going to kill that son of a bitch!"

Wilson couldn't help feeling sad. Tariq's powers seemed to impact his emotions, a burden Wilson and Takatoka didn't have to carry with theirs. Quickly, he helped Tariq wrap himself in the remaining tatters of his clothing and pulled the boys away from the area.

"Let's get out of here before Calian knows we're gone."

Takatoka looked worried.

"You want to try to teleport again?"

"No. It's too risky. But we can try to find another part of the forest to enter."

The three boys broke into a steady jog, leaving the warzone – hoping to find a way to Wilson's brother.

11

Take That

"You stupid son of a bitch!"

Julia swung the empty metal jug at her husband, hoping to take his head off. Dustin leaned back just in time to avoid the blow but could not prevent it altogether. The container crashed into his chin, knocking him on his back. Dustin had a deep gash on his chin when he stood up, dripping blood all over the kitchen floor.

"Are you out of your goddamned mind? What the hell did you hit me for?"

But Julia wasn't finished. She ran to the kitchen drawer, pulled out a large knife, and held it out for her husband to see. Dustin held up his hands and backed away.

"Hold on, Julia. Let's talk about this. What are you doing?"

"Fuck you, you filthy bastard!"

Julia slashed wildly at Dustin as he tried to back out of the room.

"Stop, Julia! Tell me what this is about!"

"Now you want to talk? After all the shit you put me through? Put our family through? Now you want to talk?"

"Look at me, Julia. I'm bleeding! Tell me what's wrong."

"Bleeding?! If I had a gun, I'd blow your fucking head off! Why are the spirits here, Dustin? Why are they all around us?"

"Is that it? Are you still afraid of ghosts? I told you the spirits are harmless!"

"I'll give you harmless, you pussy!"

Suddenly Julia threw the knife at Dustin's head. He ducked, and it stuck in the wall. Julia turned and retrieved another knife from the drawer.

"Julia, you're really starting to piss me off! Stop throwing knives and talk to me!"

"Every word out of your mouth is a goddamned lie! I can't trust a single word you say!"

"I don't know where this is coming from."

"You sick fuck! Did you make love to me in a room with your grandfather's head buried underneath the bed?"

"I....I don't know what you're talking about."

"The spirits are here because your grandfather and grandmother killed them!"

Shocked, Dustin moved closer to his wife.

"Hold on. Where did you hear that? I don't know who's been talking to you, but...."

Angered by Dustin's attempt at playing innocent, Julia pointed the blade at him once more.

"Go ahead and deny it, you sack of shit!"

"Talk to me, Julia. Your behavior is seriously scaring me."

"Okay, you want to talk? Fine! Let's talk! Talk about what's at that well that you pretend is so far away. Let's talk about that!"

Startled by Julia's words, Dustin began to stutter.

"W-w-what? What do y-y-you mean?"

"I mean, what is at that well?"

Julia was so angry she started crying. Dustin's stuttering confirmed her worst fears. He always stuttered whenever he was lying.

"I-I-I don't know w-what you mean," Dustin explained while looking down at his feet.

Julia took a step in his direction, and he jumped before moving slowly away from her.

"Let me ask you this. Do you think I'm asking about that well because I *don't* know what's going on?"

"Julia, I don't know what you have in your mind, but...."

"Stop lying! Noya isn't dead! She's at that well with her mother!"

Dustin's eyes widened.

"How do you know...."

Julia backed away from Dustin while shaking her head and wiping the tears from her eyes.

"You sick fuck. You sorry, son of a bitch!"

"Okay. Listen. It was the only way to trick Mr. Green. He had to believe that they were dead. He wouldn't...."

Julia released a fresh batch of tears and shook her head in disbelief.

"How could you let that crazy bitch lie to our sons - our family?"

"She didn't hurt the boys."

"Are you insane?! Did you not see those snakes drag Michael by his chest across the yard?!"

"Okay, but we don't know the extent of his injuries. He could be okay."

"Do you hear yourself?! How does a little boy recover from something like that?"

Dustin grew quiet.

"You let that evil bitch trick Wilson into thinking something was wrong with him, that he was an unexplainable freak of nature when she was the one that harmed his eye and put a spell on him!"

"No. That's not true. The power didn't come from mom or grandma, and no one knows where it came from."

"And you send both our sons out there in this hell?"

"We didn't have a choice, Julia. You see what's out there, and mom wasn't wrong about that."

"What kind of hold do Ama and Noya have over you? You're sick! A real man would never allow their children to put themselves in harm's way!"

Dustin lowered his eyes.

"There are things you just wouldn't understand."

"Oh, I understand perfectly. You let your twisted witch-of-a-mother convince you to experiment with our sons and send them to their deaths."

"Wilson's and Michael's paths are written in the prophecy."

Julia began laughing hysterically.

"Prophecy, huh? Let's see how prophetic all of you are when these spirits figure out that Ama and Noya have been using a spell to hold them captive as bodyguards. Let's see what happens to your asses then. In the meantime, I'm getting the fuck out of here!"

Julia grabbed a plastic bag from the counter and began shoving food inside.

"Wait! What? What are you doing?"

"Something I should've done years ago. I'm leaving!"

Dustin grabbed Julia by her arm.

"You can't just walk out there. What about that mess in the forest?"

Angrily, Julia jerked her arm away.

"All that shit about your people this and your people that! The torture of you constantly making feel like I was responsible for killing Native Americans. The years of bullshit you subjected our sons to—year after year of your subliminal brainwashing about how we should stay away from my racist family. All the holidays we missed to cater to your sensitive ego. And at the end of it all, what do I discover? My self-righteous husband's family is currently enslaving an army of spirits for personal protection. And as if that wasn't enough, my asshole of a husband has offered up both his sons as slaves to protect the witches living outback. Fuck you, Dustin! I'm leaving!"

"You're not going anywhere."

"You're half-Black, did you know that? How can you do that to your people?"

"Sure, my grandfather was Black, and Nana Ama is Cherokee, but my people are...."

Dustin stopped talking mid-sentence.

"Go ahead and finish it."

Dustin turned his back to Julia.

"This isn't helpful."

"Say it, you coward!"

"Julia..."

"*My people are Cherokee.* Go ahead and say it! That's what she's been teaching you, hasn't she? Love one half and enslave the other half, isn't that it? Ama brainwashed you into hurting your blood!"

"It's not so simple."

"Why is it that Thanksgiving offends you so much? We've invited your white colleagues over for dinner dozens of times, but Jessica and her husband? Never!"

"Stop, Julia."

"What's the matter? The truth hurts, doesn't it? It's okay for our sons to wear shoulder-length hair and perform traditional Cherokee harvest rituals, but it's not okay for the boys to invite over their Black classmates? Do young dark-skinned boys wearing baggy jeans intimidate the sensitive Cherokee, or could it be that you want to enslave them too?"

"I'm warning you. Stop!"

"Those spirits out there are part of your family! Yours and our sons'! And you're enslaving them!"

Suddenly Dustin slapped Julia and sent her tumbling to the floor.

"I'm sorry. I...."

Julia climbed to her feet and wiped the remaining tears from her eyes.

"Don't worry, Dustin. There's no romance left between us. I'm not like your grandmother. If I cut your fucking head off, it'll be to protect our sons from your bullshit."

"Protect?! You're wrong about that, Julia. I love them too! I love the boys just as much as you."

"Shut your mouth, you fucking momma's boy. You'd rather turn our sons into slaves for that bitch than to be a father to them."

"There are things you don't know about our family."

Julia smirked.

"Not that lame shit again. Please, don't make me vomit. Get the fuck out of my way! I'm going to get our sons!"

"How will you get through the forest? Where will you look? Do you know where they are?"

"All legitimate questions a concerned father would be asking in search of his sons. Oh, but wait! You're not that."

Julia walked into the bedroom and grabbed her clothes. Just as she turned to the door to leave, an old woman with tanned, leathery skin and long silver hair blocked her exit. Julia almost stopped breathing as she realized who was standing before her - it was Nana Ama, Grandma Noya's mother!

"Sleeeeeep!" the woman whispered, the irises of her eyes glowing like white coals on a fire. Julia's eyelids suddenly felt heavy, and she dropped the bag on the floor.

"Let me go to find my sons, you fucking bitch," mumbled Julia as she swayed back and forth. Dustin walked from behind the old lady and grabbed his wife's arm. Gently, he lowered her to the edge of the bed.

"Come on, baby. It would be best if you had some sleep," he whispered.

Julia fell back on the bed. She struggled mightily to keep her eyes open, but she couldn't.

"Dustin. What are they doing to me?" she asked before finally closing her eyes.

As soon as Julia fell asleep, a terrifying feeling caused her to sit up and look around. There was darkness throughout the room, and she was alone.

"Dustin? You here?" she asked, standing up.

Suddenly the face of Ama shot out of the darkness, startling Julia, knocking her to the ground.

"He's ours!" the old lady's face shrieked. "His blood is ours to do as we must!"

Julia covered her head and shrank away, terrified. She could feel the power of the old woman, pulling at her soul like a piece of loose thread on a sweater. At that moment, Julia realized the power of the family. Dustin wasn't a loving son but an obedient servant. And both of Julia's sons were tools Ama and Noya used to rip at the fabric of the world.

"I'm sorry. I'm sorry," Julia whispered over and over. But the only response she got was the laughter of Ama, her cackle echoing in Julia's head like an endlessly ringing bell. As the woman's laughter grew louder and louder, Julia lost consciousness again.

12

The Rising

"This has got to be a trick," whispered Tariq as the three boys stood on the edge of a different part of the forest. Wilson agreed. This part of the forest didn't have those strange lights flashing that they'd seen at the other location. Here, everything was silent and normal – too normal. Wilson could even hear the songs of the crickets singing.

"Should we go in?" asked Takatoka.

Wilson touched his eye and looked inside the forest. There was nothing abnormal about it that raised his alarm. Still, he couldn't help feeling something was afoot.

"I can't see anything dangerous. Let's go in, but you guys need to be ready to use your powers at first sight of trouble."

The three boys walked past the line of enormous trees and into the forest. As they moved through the darkness, dozens of fireflies flew around the boys, seemingly lighting their path as they moved.

"This is freaky," whispered Takatoka. "It's like something knows we're coming."

"Hey, Tariq. I can't see anything using my powers, but maybe you could use your powers to communicate. Wouldn't the animals be able to tell you something?" asked Wilson.

Tariq sucked his teeth in frustration.

"Nah, man. Recharging my powers takes a whole day, and I can't do anything until then."

The boys continued walking for a few minutes. It wasn't long until the thick forest gave way to weeds and sharp briars.

"Ow!" yelled Takatoka as he carefully removed a sharp briar from his shirt. "Hey Wilson, you really think your brother's in this shit? These briars are a bitch!"

Wilson didn't speak. He didn't know where he was going. All he knew was that he was running out of time to find Michael.

Suddenly Tariq stopped.

"Holy shit," exclaimed Tariq while looking up into the night sky. "You guys see that?"

Wilson looked up and was surprised to see the moon covering the night sky. It was closer to the earth than any other time he'd seen it. Suddenly a nauseous feeling overcame him, and he stopped walking to collect himself.

"Guys, I think I'm going to be sick," whispered Wilson.

The moon's closeness was surprising, but that isn't what sickened Wilson. What made him sick was what he was witnessing in the night sky. The moon seemed visually separated by two competing forces. Half of it was covered in the brilliance of sunlight, casting golden sparkles out into space; the other half looked like it had been dipped in blood, its ominous color slowly eating away at the sun-covered portion like bacteria in a petri dish.

To see such a sight made Wilson's skin crawl. The way the red light of the eclipse seemed to ooze across the surface of the moon, eating at the bright half like cancer, felt disturbing to his senses. It was one of the vilest things Wilson had ever witnessed. It was like seeing thousands of infectious puss-filled bumps rise on smooth skin before his very eyes. He quickly cleared his throat and spat into the bushes. After wiping the phlegm from the corner of his mouth, Wilson looked up again at the moon, hoping his imagination was getting the best of him. Once again, he felt disgusted at the spectacle, realizing that the vomit-inducing sight wasn't going away.

Soon a scarlet-colored light slowly crept across the forest. When the light touched Wilson's skin, he gagged. He swallowed hard as chunks of food shot into his throat from his stomach. Takatoka and Tariq watched as Wilson spat again and took in a deep breath, trying to hold the vomit down.

"Looking at the moon doesn't make the two of you feel sick?"

Tariq shrugged and continued staring at the eclipse.

"Not me. It looks kind of like cheesy bumps on the back of my uncle's neck when he uses a dirty razor."

Shaking his head in disbelief before wiping his mouth, Wilson turned to Takatoka.

"You're not feeling sick either?"

"Maybe it's something you ate. It's only an eclipse, right? Seeing the moon doesn't do anything to me. It reminds me of cottage cheese mixed with ketchup."

Frustrated by his display of weakness, Wilson started walking once more.

"Did either of you know there would be an eclipse today?" he asked.

"No, and if I did, I would've kept my ass at home," replied Tariq.

Takatoka turned and gave Tariq a skeptical look.

"What are you, a werewolf or something? Are you scared of the moon?"

"Strange things always happen during an eclipse, especially lunar ones."

"Stranger than the things we've seen so far? One of our friends turned into a one-armed monster, and that wasn't enough for you? A zombie girl attacked us with blood-sucking worms. What could be worse than that?"

"This stuff is strange, but I'm not talking about the things that scare you. I'm talking about death. Extinction level events. Like a comet crashing into the earth. The death of the dinosaurs. The plague. Things that wipe out big chunks of life on earth. All those things happened during an eclipse."

"Come on. There's no way you could know all those things happened during an eclipse."

"Idiot. Well, of course, I wasn't alive then, but my grandfather talked to the spirits. He said they told him those things happened, and I believe him. He said I'd get my powers, and I did."

The boys continued walking in silence until Wilson decided to speak.

"Why did your families send you guys here?" asked Wilson.

Tariq was the first to reply.

"Well, for my family, we knew the history of Mr. Green. There's no way to prove it, but my uncle told me he's responsible for killing three of our cousins. When my grandmother had a dream about what was approaching, they decided to send me to assist."

Takatoka spoke next.

"For me, it was mostly the same. The leader of our tribe had a vision that scared her so much that she summoned the elders. After talking it over, they decided to send the person most likely to succeed in the destruction of Mr. Green. That was me."

Suddenly Tariq stopped and dropped to the ground.

"Get down!" he whispered.

The two other boys fell on their stomachs.

"What do you see?" asked Wilson, lifting his finger to his eye. Tariq pointed through the bushes.

"Up ahead. In the clearing. You see that?"

Wilson looked ahead and saw the silhouette of a person seated on the ground.

"What is it?" asked Wilson.

"I don't know," replied Takatoka. "A ghost, maybe?"

"Is it dead?" asked Tariq.

Suddenly the figure moved and let out a barely audible groan. Takatoka and Tariq readied themselves to run away.

"Come on. Let's get out of here," whispered Tariq.

"Wait!" replied Wilson. "I think it's a kid."

"A kid?!" asked Takatoka.

All three boys raised their heads to look at the shadow.

"What if it's Calian?" asked Tariq.

"What if it's that monster girl we saw back at the property?" asked Takatoka.

Cautiously, Wilson tapped his eye and peered at the shadowy figure.

"Whatever it is, it's not a monster."

"Could it be your brother?"

Wilson's heart began pounding. It was unlikely that Mr. Green would leave his brother Michael out in the open – unless he was using him as bait.

"Let's move closer," whispered Wilson. Slowly the boys crawled on all fours until they were within a few feet of the shadow. There was very little light, and Wilson couldn't tell if the child was his brother. As he strained to get a better look at the boy's face, Wilson's knee snapped a twig.

"Who's there?" asked the boy, turning in the boys' direction. Wilson smiled. It was Michael.

"It's my brother," whispered Wilson. "I'm going to get him."

Takatoka grabbed Wilson's arm.

"Wait! What if it's a trap?"

Tariq agreed.

"Yeah. Why not kill your brother and get it over with?"

Wilson grabbed Tariq by the throat.

"That's my fucking brother, dipshit!"

Tariq grabbed Wilson's hand and pushed it away.

"Chill.... chill. I'm just saying, isn't it weird for Mr. Green to leave him out in the open like that?"

Takatoka agreed.

"You've got to admit that this does seem suspicious, Wilson. Let's look around first."

Wilson shook his head.

"Since neither of you has a kidnapped brother, we're doing this my way. Now let's go!"

A frightened Takatoka looked at Tariq and shrugged. Both the boys followed Wilson as he crawled closer to his brother. When he got within a few feet of his brother Wilson signaled for his friends to stay in their positions.

"You guys stay here. I'm going to check it out."

Wilson moved even closer to Michael. He could barely contain his emotions. It seemed like forever since he'd seen his little brother. Wilson grabbed a rock and threw it to get Michael's attention. He missed his target, and the pebble landed to the right of Michael. Wilson grabbed another stone. This time he threw it and hit the boy on the shoulder.

"Pssst. Michael!" whispered Wilson. "It's me! Wilson!"

As Michael tried to turn in his brother's direction, Wilson noticed that he could only partially move his neck. He waited patiently while Michael's terrified eyes darted around the area, searching for what had spoken to him.

"Michael!" he whispered a little louder. "It's me, Wilson!"

"Leave me alone, you sack of shit! If you're going to kill me, get it over with already! I'm sick of your fucking games!"

Wilson jumped when he heard the words come from his brother's mouth. He'd never heard Michael's voice filled with such vitriol and outright desperation. Wilson could tell the boy had moved beyond fear and was now in the realm of indifference to death.

"Michael! I'm in the bushes behind you! It's your brother!"

Finally, Michael's eyes widen in acceptance of his possible rescue.

"Wilson! Is that you?"

"Yeah. It's me!"

Wilson took a closer look at his little brother. Michael's eyes were swollen and red like he'd been unable to sleep for days. The child had tree leaves in his hair and red welts all over his body. Even from his position, Wilson could smell the strong scent of urine coming from the boy.

"We're coming to save you!"

Suddenly Michael began shaking his head back and forth frantically in protest.

"No! Don't come into the clearing!"

"Why not?"

"There's something in here! A creature, a thing. I don't know what it is, but I'm stuck. If you come in, you'll be trapped too!"

Wilson looked around the area but was unable to see anything. Once again, he whispered to Michael while Takatoka and Tariq remained silent.

"How long have you been here?"

"I don't know—a few hours. Maybe a few days. How the hell am I supposed to know? I went to sleep and woke up."

"Is it just the one creature you saw?"

"There are some monsters in the forest on the other side of the opening. But they all seem to stay away from this clearing. The thing that I saw was a shape-shifting shadow, and it came at me from the other side of the field."

"Okay. Give me a few minutes to think of a way to get you out. I'll be over here in the bushes."

"Wilson, don't you leave me! You can't! We're brothers! If you leave, I'll tell mom and dad you abandoned me!"

"Chill, Michael."

"Fuck you! I'm going to die in here! Get me out! Now!"

"Can you describe what that creature looks like?"

Michael became more hysterical as he explained what he saw.

"It's a lion! I mean, it's a buffalo. It's....it's a shadow!"

Wilson realized his mistake in asking Michael to explain how the monster looked. The boy was too hysterical to explain anything coherently. He quickly tried to calm Michael down.

"You've got to relax, Michael. You're getting too loud, and we don't know what else is in the forest."

Michael ignored Wilson and became more animated.

"Mr. Green sent some monsters after me, but I lost them! Then Grandma Noya helped me! More worms came out of my chest. But I killed everyone with the triangle. I don't know if I got Mr. Green because he's a sneaky son of a bitch!"

Wilson threw another stone at Michael, but the rock hit the boy much harder this time.

"Cut it out, Numb Nuts! If Mr. Green hears us, we're all dead!"

"But what if that thing...."

"Calm down, bro. I'm not going anywhere. I'll be here with you. Just give me a few minutes to come up with a plan on how to get you out."

Wilson crawled back over to his friends.

"Did either of you see anything?" Wilson asked while pointing to the corner of the clearing. "He said it came from over there."

"Nah, man. We haven't seen anything. Man, your brother sounds like he's out of his mind. How are we going to get him out?"

Wilson surveyed the area. After thinking for a few moments, he returned to the hiding spot closest to Michael.

"Mike!"

"Are you getting me out now? Hurry up!"

"In a second. We're still working on that."

"Working?! Hurry the fuck up! My neck and back are killing me!"

"Do you remember that trick Grandma Noya taught us when we were at the creek?"

Michael became angry.

"Trick?! Wilson, stop playing! Get me out of here!"

Wilson remained calm and patiently spoke to his little brother.

"Take a minute and think, Michael. Remember what Grandma Noya taught me to do with the mud?"

"The shapes?"

"Yeah. The shapes. Since we don't know where that thing is hiding, and we're not sure what's holding you down, let me try to move the ground around you. Maybe that will free you. I think it's worth a shot."

Michael's breathing returned to normal.

"Okay. Do it."

Wilson turned to crawl back to Takatoka and Tariq when Michael called out to him.

"Hey, Wilson!"

"Yeah? I'm here."

"What if it doesn't work?"

"If it doesn't, we have another option. Don't worry. I'm not leaving this place without you."

"Thanks, Wilson. I love you."

The sudden display of affection caught Wilson off guard. His eyes filled with water as he backed away from his little brother.

"I love you too, little brother. Don't worry. We're coming for you."

As soon as Wilson got back to Tariq and Takatoka, he laid out their plan.

"We may be able to free Michael without stepping into the clearing," explained Wilson.

"How?" asked Takatoka.

Wilson closed his eyes and shoved both palms into the black soil.

"We may be able to free Michael using a trick my grandmother showed me. I'm able to loosen the dirt around him without getting close. Maybe he'll be able to break free."

Tariq shook his head.

"I doubt that's going to work. Your brother doesn't seem to be attached to the ground. Whatever's holding him there is supernatural."

"Do either of you have any better ideas? Because outside of running full force onto that field to grab Michael, this is the only option I have....well that or sending an invisible Takatoka out there to try to grab him."

"Me? Why me? We don't even know what's out there," whispered Takatoka in protest.

"Chickenshit," laughed Tariq.

Wilson shoved his hands even deeper into the dirt.

"Shut up, you guys! I need to concentrate."

The boys turned their attention to Wilson's brother seated in the clearing. Suddenly the grass around him began to tremble slightly. Next, clumps of dirt began rising from the ground and moving away from Michael.

"It's working!" whispered Michael as he watched chunks of dirt move away from him.

Wilson focused harder. Soon much larger chunks of the ground began moving away from Michael. It wasn't long before a large pit had formed in a circle around the boy. Michael began wriggling.

"I still can't move!" he yelled, desperately trying to free himself. Hearing his brother's complaints made Wilson concentrate even more. Soon vast pieces of the ground rose from the ground and flew to the opposite side of the field.

"Wilson! Stop!" whispered Takatoka.

"You're out of control!" yelled Tariq.

But Wilson never heard them. He was so focused on freeing his little brother that Wilson didn't consider the amount of noise he was making – or the damage he was doing.

"Wilson!" Michael suddenly yelled. "Heeeeeelp!"

The sound of his brother's voice brought Wilson back to reality. Quickly, he removed his hands from the dirt. There was a rush of air, and then Wilson heard the worst sound he'd ever heard in his life - the sound of Michael's voice trailing away.

"AAAAAAAHHHH!"

Wilson stood and looked out onto the field.

"Oh no!" Wilson exclaimed.

A giant sinkhole had formed in the place where Michael had been sitting. His brother was gone!

Wilson took off running.

"Hey! Wait!" yelled Tariq. "Takatoka, grab him!"

Takatoka reached to grab Wilson's sleeve but was a few inches too late. He missed.

"Wilson! No!" Takatoka yelled after him. But the boy was out of reach. Wilson scurried towards the clearing with his eyes focused on the edge of the sinkhole.

"Oh my God! Oh no!" Wilson whispered. If Michael were dead, there would be no way he would ever be able to forgive himself.

Wilson ran onto the field, determined to pull his little brother from the hole before the walls caved in and buried him alive. As soon as his foot touched the grass, his whole body became stiff.

"Whaaaat....is thisssss?" he asked in slurred tongue while drool suddenly began pouring from his mouth. He lifted his foot to take a step.

"AAAAAAGGHH!" he screamed. His leg felt like it weighed a thousand pounds. Wilson reached down to try to grab the heavy leg with both hands but was shocked to see his fingers; curled like an old man's; the joints swollen and thick with arthritic pain so excruciating that he couldn't move them.

"T...Takatoka!" he yelled. "Tariq!"

But no one came to his rescue.

Soon a terrifying thought entered his mind. What if his brother hadn't survived the fall in the pit?

"Michael!" Wilson yelled, his voice trembling with fear and adrenaline. He tried to listen for any sound coming from within the sinkhole. But there was nothing.

"Michael! Answer me!"

But there was still no response.

Suddenly Wilson felt a powerful force hit him squarely in the small of his back, causing him to fly through the air.

"AAAAAHHHGGG!" Wilson screamed as pain shot through his spine. Unable to lift his hands to break his fall, he landed face-first in the dirt. He tried to roll over to see what was happening, but the pressure pushed down hard on his back once more, making him feel like a bug on the bottom of a shoe. Wilson couldn't move.

"Hey! Heeeeelp!" Wilson managed to scream. Suddenly he felt something grab his hair and yank his head back, making his neck pop.

"Ow! That hurts! Let go of me!" Wilson yelled. The force slammed Wilson's face into the ground and began grinding down on the back of his head. Soon Wilson was unable to breathe. He squeezed his eyes shut as he felt the small stones and sticks in the soil grind against his face.

"Why are you doing...." Wilson tried to ask. But his words were muffled by the dirt pouring into his mouth. Fearing that he'd be buried alive, Wilson struggled once more to free his arms, but he was still unable to move his body. Soon Wilson became drowsy. Dirt began entering his nose, and he couldn't push it out. Wilson could feel unconsciousness stealing on him.

Just when he'd accepted his fate, something grabbed him by the ankles and snatched Wilson out of the dirt, sending him crashing into a large tree, cracking his ribs.

"Ugh..." he gargled, unable to yell out in pain because of the mud in his mouth. Wilson took in a shallow breath and winced.

"Please! Stop!" he yelled as pain radiated across his chest. Wilson could feel the bone of his broken rib pressing against his torso. He knew if he moved too much, the bone would tear through his skin. Wilson decided to appeal to his captor, but he was flying through the air again before he could speak.

"Oh! Shiiiit!" he screamed, trying to brace himself for the pain before he landed. He landed hard on his cracked ribs in front of the sinkhole.

"AAAHHHH!" he yelled out in agony. "PLEASE STOP! I CAN'T TAKE ANY MORE!"

After lying motionless for a few seconds, Wilson waited in fear for his next bout of torture. He tried to move his arms and was surprised to find that he could move them freely. But nothing grabbed him. Wilson quickly wiped the mud from his eyes and looked around. He was alone.

"Michael!" he yelled "Takatoka! Tariq!"

He climbed to his feet and spun in circles. He touched his eye and peered into the forest, but nothing was there. Michael was gone, and his two friends were missing, leaving Wilson all alone in the field.

Suddenly a pungent odor rushed into Wilson's nostrils.

"What the fuck is that?" he asked. Wilson began coughing and wheezing. His damaged rib was making it impossible to breathe. He tried taking smaller breaths to minimize the pain in his torso, but even in tiny breaths, the smell was disgusting. Wilson was sure he'd encountered it before. He racked his brain until finally, he identified the smell.

"Bile and mud," whispered Wilson, doubling over in pain as he coughed once more. He'd smelled the same aroma at Grandma Noya's house when she'd gone out back and slaughtered a pig. The smell ruined his whole summer that year as it seemed to cling to his senses like glue.

Wilson stumbled to the edge of the sinkhole and looked inside. The hole was deep, and he could see nothing but darkness.

"Michael!" he yelled. "Can you hear me?"

Wilson got down on his knees to see if he could hear breathing from inside.

"Michael! You there?" Wilson yelled once more.

He stuck his head over the side of the hole and took in a deep breath. The smell of decaying clay filled his lungs, and Wilson gratefully let out a sigh of relief; the odor of death wasn't coming from where his brother had been.

"He's still alive," Wilson whispered as he painfully raised himself to his feet. "Gotta find him."

Like a detective, Wilson started concentrating on tracking down his brother. He looked around the clearing for any signs that his brother had escaped the fall. No footprints were leading away from the hole.

Next, Wilson remembered what Michael had told him about the shape-shifting creature he'd encountered. While holding his ribs, Wilson limped around the edge of the clearing. He was careful not to look at anything directly; realizing that shadows sometimes played tricks on the vision, Wilson thought it best to use his peripheral. After searching for a while, he found nothing.

"I know you're here, little bro. Just tell me where you are," Wilson whispered.

Suddenly warm, putrid air thick with the same stench he'd smelled earlier blew down on top of Wilson's head. Wilson slowly looked up, realizing that he'd failed to search the sky above him.

"Oh my God!" he whispered.

The eclipse was nearly complete; aside from a small piece of the surface, the moon was red, blanketed in the horrible bloody sludge that made Wilson sick to his stomach. But Wilson couldn't look away. There was something on the moon's surface that hadn't been visible the first time he'd looked - a large bloody hoof print.

Fearing what he might see, Wilson ran his finger across his eyelid and slowly looked up once more. He saw two giant glowing animal eyes staring down at him as soon as he did.

Terrified, Wilson quickly deactivated his powers and stumbled backward, landing on his back.

"Shit!" he cursed, feeling the pain of his broken rib as it moved unrestrained inside his torso.

Suddenly the trees all around the clearing started shaking violently. Wheezing from injured ribs, Wilson rolled over and climbed to his knees.

"Michael!" Wilson screamed. "Anybody!"

The trees surrounding the clearing began glowing from within and suddenly burst into flame. Wilson could feel the heat from the fires burning his face like a hot iron. Within seconds a blister appeared on his chin, then both his cheeks, then his forehead. He tried to move away from the fire, but the whole forest seemed to be aflame, and there was no place for him to hide. The fires from the trees intensified, growing higher and higher, seemingly warming the very air Wilson was breathing. Wilson searched the clearing, looking for a piece of the forest that wasn't burning, but everything was ablaze.

Still, the flames climbed higher into the night sky, reaching out to the moon like fingers of hell. The forest fire sucked the oxygen from the field, and Wilson crashed to the ground gasping for air. The smoke around him was like a blanket of cotton, suffocating him to death.

Suddenly the flames all converged into one tube of fire and shot into the sky. The final blast hit the center of the hoof imprint causing it to glow an eery fluorescent green. With the forest fire extinguished, Wilson could breathe again. He climbed to his knees and began coughing. Ignoring the pain from his rattling ribs, he took a welcome breath of cool air.

"None of you belong here!" a deep voice boomed from the sky.

"Wh….what?" asked Wilson, wanting to run but afraid to stand.

"Trespasser!" the voice boomed once more.

Suddenly a large animal skull burst through the soil underneath Wilson's hand. He screamed as two of his fingers sank into the enormous eye cavities of the head. Wilson struggled to remove the skull from his hand. He reached out to grab the skeletal remains with his other hand and watched in horror as the skull head opened its mouth and bit off his fingers.

"AAAAAHHHH!" Wilson screamed as blood sprayed everywhere. Before Wilson could shout again, another skull burst through the soil and clamped down on the remaining fingers of his injured hand. The two large animal skulls began glowing a bright red emitting a metallic sound as they rose into the sky, pulling Wilson off the ground.

"We will have our revenge by killing you all!" the voice echoed. "Death! Unrelenting carnage! May you all suffer the fate of those you have tormented!"

Terrified, Wilson closed his eyes and screamed into the night sky.

"What do you want?"

A metallic sound rang out that made Wilson's ears start dripping blood.

"Do you dare to question us?"

Wilson wasn't afraid anymore. He was pissed.

"I deserve to know why you're doing this to me!"

"Silence! The only right you possess is of revenge upon your bloody carcass!"

"Where's my brother?"

There was nothing but silence as Wilson drew closer to the moon. "Where is Michael?"

Suddenly the two animal skulls let go of both of Wilson's arms, and he began falling back to earth.

"Where is my brother?" Wilson yelled as he tumbled head over heels through the night sky. The only response the voice provided was a deep cackle that vibrated Wilson's cracked rib and made him moan in pain.

As the ground drew closer, Wilson looked down and saw the ground; thousands of skulls lay all over it.

"Where is my fucking brother?" he yelled once more as he prepared to die upon impact. Before hitting the ground, Wilson closed his eyes and thought of his family. He remembered all the moments he'd shared with Michael when they were at Grandma Noya's house. Wilson recalled the smell of his mother's neck, light perfume mixed with the sweat of her workday as she embraced him as soon as Wilson and Michael arrived home from school. He tried to think of his father's face but didn't have enough time. He slammed headfirst into the field of bones, erasing all thoughts from his mind.

Wilson expected to only see black after slamming into the ground, but instead, the skulls in the clearing numbered more than thousands; there were millions of them. Like an ocean, the bones softened Wilson's impact, only scratching his legs as they poked through his pants. Instead, the bones were like quicksand; they created a suction effect that pulled him down towards the bottom of the pile.

Wilson looked down as something pulled him to the bottom of the mountain of bones. He was afraid Michael had taken the same path and hoped to prepare himself for whatever was waiting. There was light shining up through the skeletal remains, casting a scary glow on the old bones yet making it easy to see every mark, every crack, every imperfection on every head.

Some of the bones whispered to Wilson as he descended:

You are not welcome!

The path to hell begins with your murder.
Blood is on your hands.

They screamed at him:

Die!
We will have our revenge!
You killed my baby!

Some skulls cried like newborns, while others barked at him like rabid dogs. Still, Wilson's descent was neverending, a fall filled with pain and judgment he couldn't comprehend. The bones ripped at Wilson's skin and clothing as he got sucked deeper.

Eventually, the skulls became soft and spongy. Wilson reached out and tried to stop his descent but found that the bones had become slippery. Long tubular objects darted into and out of the eye sockets of the skulls like serpents. Soon, the tubes attacked Wilson's legs, arms, face, and neck. They seemed to be trying to hold onto him.

Wilson gagged as the slimy objects rubbed against his face. Along with the smell that had invaded his senses earlier, there were other smells – blood, feces, and urine. Wilson tried to turn away, but more objects pushed against his face as soon as he did. The stench became more dominant. It permeated every aspect of his descent. Soon fluids flooded Wilson's mouth, and he realized that his nose hadn't failed him. He was in a pit filled with every disgusting bodily fluid he could ever imagine. Finally, a light went off in Wilson's head, and he began convulsing. He finally figured out what the gross long tubular objects were. They were animal entrails. And they were living, wriggling around his body, trying to hold on to him as he fell. Wilson finally realized where he was; he'd been consumed and was in the intestines of some giant creature.

Finally, he blacked out.

13

The Eclipse

Julia sat in a chair on the lawn, watching the explosions at the edge of the forest. She could hear the screams of thousands of strange unearthly creatures trying to come onto the property. Although a few of the hideous creatures had briefly shown themselves, they never got close to being able to go onto the property - vaporized as soon as they penetrated the invisible barrier that separated the land from the forest.

Sitting beside Julia on the lawn was her husband, Dustin. Although he, too, watched the forest nervously, his primary reason for being by Julia's side was to watch her movements, making sure she didn't slip the restraints that bound her wrists. Julia couldn't even look at him. The hatred she felt towards her husband was too great. All she could do was grind her teeth and concentrate on which part of the forest would give her the least resistance when she tried to escape.

Finally, Dustin turned to speak to her.

"You hungry? I can go make us a couple of tuna sandwiches if you'd like."

Julia ignored him. Dustin sat in silence for a moment. After a few minutes passed, he tried to engage his wife in conversation once more.

"You have to go to the bathroom? It's been a few hours, and I know you have to pee."

Still, Julia gave him no response. Dustin sighed and fell back into his chair.

"It's not that bad, Julia. Everything's going to be okay. You'll see."

Julia turned to Dustin and smiled.

"Get fucked, you spineless prick."

Slightly embarrassed, Dustin cracked a small smile before looking up into the night sky.

"Look at that moon. It's weird. Have you ever seen something so freaky?"

Julia looked up into the sky and felt excitement rush through her body. The moon was almost entirely red. She remembered what Hakim had told her about the eclipse. Soon she would be able to make her escape.

Dustin turned back towards the house and yelled.

"Hey, Mom! Did you know there would be an eclipse tonight?"

His mother, Noya, sitting in a rocking chair on the front porch, finally stood and walked out onto the lawn. Aside from red eyes and crow's feet at the corners of her eyes, Noya looked as she always did. She wore dirt-covered shorts with a stained blouse. She wasn't wearing makeup, yet her tanned skin was without blemish. A long ponytail that stretched down her back.

Julia frowned angrily at the woman, hoping to get her attention. Noya didn't take the bait. She walked into the yard and stopped several feet away from Julia and Dustin, careful not to get too close, avoiding eye contact. Casually, she looked up at the sky and then shrugged.

"No, I didn't know about it. But it doesn't matter. One moon is the same as any other."

Just as Noya turned to walk back to the porch, her mother, Ama, walked around the corner of the house. Julia watched in astonishment as the 100-year-old woman walked unassisted, upright, and as vibrant as a 50-year-old. Her long, silver hair was beautiful and fell on her shoulders like silk as she walked. All 6 feet of the woman's body were as straight as an arrow, untouched by old age. While Ama maintained the one blind eye, she didn't seem to have any trouble seeing. Julia noticed the pain that had kept Ama bedridden for years was suddenly gone.

Walking casually beside Ama was the spirit of Paul. He wore ragged, soiled clothing, and his head was balding. Although he was dead, he seemed as happy as ever. He chewed on a corncob pipe as he walked, yanking with one hand on his kinky gray beard.

Julia sat mesmerized by the couple. The times she'd seen Paul roaming about the property, he looked like a lonely old man stolen by death. But now, walking beside Ama, he seemed vibrant and full of vigor, while in comparison, she seemed too old for *him*. As the couple walked, Paul continuously tried to grab Ama's hand, only to have his hand pass through hers without contact. The attempt at affection sparked curiosity in Julia. She wondered if Paul truly loved his wife or if Ama had somehow tricked Paul into eternal servitude.

The more Julia watched the couple, the angrier she became. In all her years of marriage to Dustin, this was the first time she'd ever seen Ama standing upright. All the summers they'd sent the boys down to help out with Ama's seemingly deteriorating health had been a giant ruse.

"Fucking bitch!" Julia whispered under her breath.

She remembered when Dustin drove her to meet his family for the first time. She remembered how terrifyingly frail the woman seemed to be, making such an impression upon Julia that she returned to the property on consecutive weekends to empty the old woman's pee-pan and give her sponge baths. Julia couldn't understand why she felt such sympathy for the woman at the time. Julia's family didn't get sponge baths, so why was Julia doing it for Nana Ama? Now everything was clear. Ama's one white blind eye witched the unsuspecting young girl through the shadows in the bedroom. She cast spells that made Julia change bedsheets and scrub every floor in that old house. Ama lying in darkness, emptying her bladder onto the bedsheets, had all been part of their game – their plan. The old woman pissing on herself had intentionally kept the lie believable. Aside from the blind eye, nothing was wrong with Ama's health. Now Julia saw Ama for what she was – a witch with a plan to make her children her slaves.

"Hello, Nana Ama!" Dustin yelled, respectfully standing to greet his grandmother. Ama smiled, casting a freakishly scary glance at Julia, making her knees knock in fear. Julia tried to hide her fear and quickly looked away. Ama lifted a palm to Paul, causing him to drift back. Ama moved closer to Julia and spoke.

"Hellooooo, Juliaaaaa."

Julia almost screamed when she heard Ama's voice. Her voice was deep and airy, like it was coming from inside a hole while at the same time rattling like a can of spray paint.

Dustin turned to his wife.

"Say hello, Baby. Nana Ama doesn't speak much."

Julia lunged at her husband and tried to hit him in the face with her bound hands. He ducked and wrapped both his arms around her.

"I'm sorry, Nana. My wife's a little out of control right now."

Julia tried breaking free, hitting Dustin repeatedly in the chest with both hands.

"Let me go, you bastard!"

"When you calm down, I will. Then we can discuss the boys."

The words caused a break in Julia's fury, and she stopped swinging.

"The boys? What about the boys?"

"We can discuss how they can be a bigger help to the family."

"Listen, Dustin. You keep those deranged bitches away from our sons!"

"There's nothing you can do about it, Julia. Nana Ama says it's their destiny."

Julia started sobbing.

"What kind of a man are you?" she asked, falling to the ground.

"He's the kind of man we raised him to be - obedient, strong, and selfless. We'll make sure Wilson and Michael will share those traits. But they can only gain that strength in service to our family. Not the...."

Suddenly an explosion rang out in the sky, and everyone looked up. Julia looked up to see that the eclipse was complete. The blood-red moon that had been faraway moments earlier had drawn close to the earth.

As if every creature within the forest suddenly disappeared, the woods became silent.

"Nana!" yelled Dustin. "What's happening?"

The old woman took a few steps and looked up at the moon.

"Gigage nvda!" Ama whispered. Julia was terrified at Ama's appearance; her white eye was now glowing red from the moon's scarlet light, making the old woman seem possessed.

"Red moon," repeated Dustin, looking at a terrified Noya. "What should we do, mom?"

Noya ran down from the porch.

"This is a moon of death."

The ground began trembling violently, slamming everyone into the yard except Ama, who continued standing as she stared grimacing at the moon. After seeing Noya fall face-first to the ground, Dustin ran to his mother's aid.

"Mama!" he yelled, helping her climb to her knees.

Suddenly a high-pitched noise sounded that made everyone cover their ears.

"What is it?" asked Noya.

Everyone looked up and watched in astonishment as a white burning fire moved across the surface of the moon, raising a small cloud of red dust. Something seemed to be carving a symbol into the moondust.

"What is it?" asked Dustin, moving closer to his mother.

While everyone else stared into the sky, Julia eyed the forest and slowly inched away from the group.

"Yanasi!" whispered Ama.

Dustin appeared confused.

"A buffalo? What does it mean?"

Ama turned to Dustin and Noya and screamed.

"Run!"

Dustin searched for Julia, but he couldn't find her.

"Julia!" he screamed, turning in circles. Finally, he looked toward the edge of the forest and saw his wife entering the treeline. Julia took one look back at the group before removing the ropes from her wrists.

"Julia! Don't!" Dustin yelled.

But his wife was beyond his reach. Dustin ran to his grandmother's side.

"Nana Ama, can you do something? She'll die out there!"

Ama extended her hand and pointed in Julia's direction.

"Oyohusa!" she hissed.

Julia took one look back and disappeared into the bushes.

Noya ran to her son's side and grabbed him by the arm.

"Come on, son. We've got to get out of here!"

Just as she turned to leave, a laser beam of red light shot out from the moon and hit Noya in the center of her forehead.

"Mama!" Dustin yelled, reaching out to grab his mother's arm. Noya's eyes and hair turned black. Slowly, she rose into the air, convulsing and thrashing. Eventually, her body went limp, and her arms fell to her side. Her mouth opened wide to reveal that she'd bitten off her tongue and was choking on the blood, a strange sound vibrating in her throat.

"Uggghghghg…"

Suddenly the light lifted her out of her son's reach and pulled Noya towards the moon.

"Mom! Come back!" Dustin yelled, jumping helplessly at his mom's feet. Finally, he turned back to his retreating grandmother.

"Nana Ama! Do something!"

Ama looked back briefly at her grandson before turning to continue her retreat. She was halfway across the yard when a separate red light struck her from behind, sending her flying into the air and keeping her there, suspended in animation. The laser was so intense that it split her skull into halves. The exposed brain began to throb and bubble up out of Ama's skull, eventually becoming so big that the other parts of the woman's head cracked and leaked fluid down the sides of her face. The red light of the eclipse turned Ama's exposed brain black like a dirty spongecake. Her eyes also became black, and her throat produced the same mechanical sounds as Noya's before she finally took flight towards the moon.

Dustin fell to the ground and watched in horror.

"Why is this happening?"

Soon Noya and Ama were so high in the sky that they were out of his reach. Sensing the eclipse wasn't done, Dustin ran to the back of the house and disappeared into the weeds.

Paul's Fate

12:02 am:

"Come home to me, my love."

The spirit of Paul sat on the edge of the bed with an old, dirt-covered skull in his lap, staring at the bedroom door. It didn't bother him that the head was his. It only mattered that Ama had kept it, a testament to the promise they'd made to one another long ago.

"I miss holding you, my sweet Ama," he whispered, fingering the eye sockets of his head while waiting for his love to appear. Paul thought back to just a few moments earlier when he walked across the lawn with his wife. It was one of his favorite things to do. He took such joy in being able to see her smile in the moonlight.

But although he was happy to be able to see his wife, Paul felt a certain melancholy at the moment; the impossibility of touching her tortured him; He was dead, and she wasn't.

And in the blink of an eye, everything changed.

As if empathizing with Paul's torture, something reached down from the heavens and struck his wife in the face, killing her dead. Everything had seemed to be happening in slow motion: there was a blood-colored flash of light; her skull splitting open; Ama floating in the air, the whites of her eyes black and empty; a faraway look plastered on her face.

At the time, Paul didn't feel sadness or shock at the violent manner in which Ama passed. He only felt a sense of complete and utter joy.

Paul immediately disappeared and reappeared in their bedroom, not waiting to see the outcome. He was so happy he could barely contain himself. His wife was dead, and soon she'd be back in his arms. Nothing pleased him more than the thought of their reunion.

And now he was here he was, in their old bedroom, waiting for their inevitable reconnection.

As he sat waiting for Ama, Paul let his mind wander. He thought back to the last day he'd touched his wife – the day they returned to their home after killing the sharecroppers. Although the moment was dreadful, it was a moment he cherished.

"Are you sure this is going to work?" Paul asked.

"It will if we maintain our plans," responded Ama.

The young woman got up from the table and walked to the bedroom. When she returned, she carried a small black book with a golden symbol on the cover.

"I've planned everything. Don't worry."

"And you're sure about this."

"I am."

Paul rubbed the symbol on the book with his index finger. He didn't know anything about witchcraft and sorcery, but Paul figured anything was possible after seeing Mr. Green and all he could do. The only thing Paul was sure of was his love for Ama. He believed in her with all his soul.

Finally, he stood up and picked up the machete from the floor.

"Did you enjoy dinner?" asked Ama.

"I did. It was special," replied Paul.

Ama beckoned for her husband to come to her. As soon as he did, she grabbed his hand and kissed it.

"You have to leave now."

"You're not coming with me?"

"Who'll take care of Noya?"

Paul sighed and looked at his daughter sleeping on the floor.

"You're right."

"Don't worry. It may take a little time, but we'll be together again. I promise."

Paul kissed Ama gently on her forehead.

"The day will come when I leave this realm. Death happens to us all, and I'm no exception to that rule. Your spirit will be close to me when death takes me. When that happens, run to the bedroom and dig up the floorboards."

"Why? What will be there?"

"A part of you."

Paul smiled.

"A part of me? Which part?"

"Don't be disgusting about it. Just know that no other man will warm our bed."

Paul kissed his wife once more.

"Are you ready?" he asked, handing the machete to Ama.

"I am," she responded coldly, nodding towards the table.

Paul walked back to his seat and sat down in his chair. With a smile on his face, he laid his head down on the table and closed his eyes. Ama walked up behind him and kissed his neck.

"Remember to check the floorboards underneath the bed. Do not forget to retrieve what I leave for you. It will be the only way I'll know it's you."

With both hands, Ama lifted the large knife high. The candlelight flashed on the blade of the machete, but Paul never saw it. He'd briefly closed his eyes in fear, unsure of pain's association with death. But just as the blade cut through Paul's neck, he reopened his eyes and watched as his head tumbled away from the table. Paul had never seen such a loving look on his wife's face as was present within that moment. As his head landed on the floor with a thud, Paul smiled. Although his head had fallen away from his body, he could still see his baby daughter Noya sleeping peacefully on the floor – next to his decapitated head.

1:15 am:

Minutes passed, and then an hour. Still, Ama did not appear.

Paul chewed on his pipe and waited patiently. Suddenly, he started laughing heartily.

"Even in death, this woman is going to make me wait."

Paul stood and walked to the frail nightstand by the bed. With his foot, he tried kicking the rickety contraption, only to watch his shoe pass through it. Amused and somewhat disappointed by the act, Paul walked over to the bed and tried sitting down on it. Just as he had done earlier, he floated partially between the mattress and on top of it, telling himself that he was sitting. But Paul wasn't sitting. Air moved through him like a feather in a breeze, and he had to exert a little concentration to prevent himself from falling through the floor. Paul didn't know how he learned how to stay in place, but he knew how to move on this plane of existence, just as all the other spirits knew.

2:40 am:

Paul could feel anxiety creeping into the room.

"Where is she?" he asked, standing and letting the skull fall to the floor. Thus far, their plan worked out just as Ama said it would. It wasn't like Ama to be late. In their married life, Ama was such a stickler for punctuality that she'd stopped talking to him for a month when he'd been thirty minutes late coming home from the fields. And now she was missing? Could she have forgotten a crucial detail?

3:20 am:

Paul walked over to the bedroom door and stood in front of it. Hesitantly, he took a step and stuck his hand out, watching calmly as his hand passed through the wood.

"Where are you, my Ama?" he asked in desperation. There was a hunger deep inside that Paul wanted, no, *needed* extinguished. Ama had promised as soon as she died, her spell would pull her to Paul. But it hadn't happened. Although he'd watched the red light split his wife's head open and kill her, Ama hadn't come to him. He'd waited for hours for his wife, and still - nothing.

Fearing Ama needed help, Paul prepared to push the rest of his body through the door when he suddenly stopped. He'd forgotten his skull on the floor next to the bed.

"Ama might be in trouble," Paul said as he pushed more of his arm through the door. Paul would do his best to be there if his wife needed him. After all, why did he need to carry around that old skull? It was ridiculous. He was dead, and there was no need for a dusty old head in the afterlife.

Suddenly, Ama's voice echoed in his head:

"It will be the only way I'll know it's you."

Paul pulled his arm back, walked over to the skull lying on the floor, and picked it up.

"She won't know me if I'm not carrying this thing," he said, tucking the head under his arm.

Paul walked back to the door and paused with his skeletal remains in hand, realizing that he could easily pass through the door, but the skull couldn't.

"Goddamned ghost rules."

Frustrated by his inability to carry the remains through the door, Paul returned to the bed and sat down.

"Maybe someone will enter soon."

But Paul knew no one was coming to open the door, at least not from the living world. The truth was, Paul was expecting his wife. Only her. He wanted to stay in that room, waiting for Ama just as they'd planned. He fantasized about her spirit bursting through the door filled with passion. Free from the constraints of life, the couple would consummate their newfound eternity together by making love for days. Weeks. Months. Years. The house was in the forest, and no one could hear them. If someone did stumble upon the rotted structure, they'd be afraid of the sounds coming from the house. But the truth would be that Paul and his wife were celebrating their marriage together -reunited after a lifetime apart.

3:45 am:

"Goddamn it, woman! Where are you?"

Paul stood and glared at the bedroom door.

"If I had a bedroom window, I wouldn't be going through this mess!" he snapped, angry at the fact that it was Ama who'd suggested a window in the bedroom, and it was he who rejected the idea. Once again, Paul let the skull fall to the floor, this time dislocating the jawbone, sending it sliding to the other side of the room. As he looked at the partially broken skull, he became terrified at the damage he'd caused and shot through the air to scoop the remains off the floor.

"No...no....no," he said over and over, trying desperately to piece the skull back together. Finally, Paul heard a click and the jawbone reconnected.

"Thank God!" he exhaled, placing the skull gently on the bed beside him. As he sat watching the cranium, surveying it for damages, a thought popped into his mind.

"I am such a dumb bastard," he said, doubling over in laughter. It had been so long since he'd died that Paul forgot the path he'd taken. To walk as a ghost among the living, a soul had to travel to the Field of Souls. Paul remembered his trip there and how he'd encountered Hakim, the fat gatekeeper. Hakim's job was to guide all deceased to their waiting place in the Field of Souls until they passed on to their new plane of existence. Paul remembered how disgusted he'd been when he met the man, his huge belly and disgusting odor thick in the air.

But Paul never made it there. Just as Hakim doused Paul in a strange fluid, Paul disappeared – sucked out of the world of the undead and brought back to the realm of the living by Ama, who had discovered a spell to cheat death and get her husband back to her world. Still, Paul had no way of knowing exactly how long the process was.

"Maybe it takes a few hours," he told himself.

And so, Paul continued waiting.

4:30 am:

Paul was sitting on the bed inspecting his head when he heard a whisper out in the hall.

"Paaaaaul."

Surprised, Paul again dropped the skull on the floor, sending the jawbone sprawling anew.

"Ama? Is that you?"

Paul gathered the pieces of his bone and quickly moved across the room to the bed.

"I'm in here, baby. I'm in our bedroom."

Paul didn't bother with trying to piece the head together again. He just sat the bone on the bed with the jaw loosely balancing underneath it.

"Paaaaaul," the voice whispered again.

"Ama! I'm in here!" Paul yelled, alternating from various positions within the room to best receive his wife.

"Paaaaaul."

Paul became a little unnerved after hearing the voice call his name a third time.

"Ama, is it you?" he asked. "Are you there?"

To Paul, hearing his wife speak his birth name was weird – creepy even. Although the voice sounded vaguely like his wife, Paul couldn't be sure it was her. Ama wasn't a woman of many words. The silence was something she'd learned as a little girl in her Cherokee tribe; the elders were strict on children listening instead of being loud. In his many years of marriage to Ama, he'd only heard her soft, deep voice in the most private of settings. She was careful only to speak to Paul, and she never allowed others to listen to what they shared.

"That voice...." Paul whispered.

What he heard out in the hall sounded like it belonged to a young person – a child even. There was an iciness to it that froze Paul's thoughts, drenching them in doubt, making him hate himself for not being more learned of the woman sharing his last name. The voice floating down the hallway felt unromantic. Foreign. Terrifyingly emotionless, cloaking the things that made conversation feel regular and fluid in a shroud of doubt and fear. The speech was a repellant to Paul, and he couldn't figure out why his wife sounded so – vengeful.

Paul took one final look at the skull lying on the bed and then moved to the bedroom door.

"If she's out there, I can quickly come back in to grab it," he whispered, deciding to go out to search for his wife. He was scared now. His wife didn't sound the same.

When Paul moved through the door, the sensation felt like all the other times - the feeling of eucalyptus and soda bubbling on the bridge of his nose, and then he was through. But as soon as he stepped into the hallway, a dark, brooding feeling overcame Paul with such force that he started trembling. Soon he was sweating, unable to understand why fear, something he hadn't felt since death, was suddenly upon him. Something evil was there in the hallway with him – and it wasn't his wife.

Paul quickly turned and looked down the hall. There was nothing there but an old dresser covered in dust. Feeling relieved, Paul turned and looked down the other end of the hall. Standing just beyond the hallway in the living room was the shadow of a little girl, her eyes seemingly glowing white as she stood, staring at him. Paul squinted and thought he recognized the child. It was Brenda, one of the spirits. The child ran around the land, laughing and playing with her mother. When they killed the sharecroppers, Brenda had been one of their first victims.

"Brenda, where's your mom?" Paul asked as he moved towards the child. Suddenly a tall woman stepped out of the shadows and stood by the little girl. Paul stopped and stared at the woman, unable to see her shadowed face. He could only assume it was Brenda's mother.

"Did you see the eclipse?" Paul asked, trying to pretend everything was normal. Other than the terrifying feeling that he had in the center of his chest, everything *was* normal. Paul had seen the mother and daughter numerous times, and they'd seen him. He was unafraid of the two because just as Ama's spell had done with all the others, their memories were wiped clean. The mother and child's nonresponse didn't feel weird or out of place. Most of the spirits roamed around in a half zombie-like daze, a feature that Paul's conscience deeply appreciated, with him being responsible for the deaths roaming the property.

Suddenly the woman walked to the small table sitting in front of them and lit a candle. The sight of the child terrified Paul. Brenda's lips were purple and twisted back on her teeth. Small purplish veins traced through her gray face and her brown eyes bulged, partially dislodged from her eye sockets.

"No!" Paul screamed.

It was a face Paul had seen before – the night he'd choked the little girl to death after killing her father in the fields.

"It can't be! How did you...."

Paul's eyes fell on the uncloaked figure standing beside Brenda – it was Cynthia, the little girl's mother! From the bridge of her nose to her bottom lip was a deep indentation in the woman's skull. And Paul remembered why. She'd walked in on Paul just as he'd finished killing little Brenda. The mother took one look at her dead little girl and immediately began raining down blows on the back of Paul's head, sending him sprawling face-first towards the hot fireplace. If not for a large stone to the side of the fireplace, Paul would've fallen into the fire. Instead, he pushed off the large rock and fell on his side. Cynthia lept on Paul's chest and attempted to stab him in the eyes with a hot poker, but she missed when Paul hit Cynthia with a blow to her face. Paul lept to his feet and grabbed the first weapon he could find - the stone. When he smashed it into the woman's face, blood squirted all over the room.

"Paaaaaul," Brenda whispered. "Weeeee know what you've done."

Brenda extended her arm and pointed at Paul, her index finger broken from fighting the man for her life.

"Theeee others knoooow," whispered the mother, taking a step in Paul's direction. As soon as she did, one of her grayed eyeballs fell out of her damaged skull and hit the floor.

Suddenly, Brenda started crying. Her tiny voice echoing in the hall was the most painful sound Paul had ever heard. He cupped his ear and backed away.

"But....Ama said. How?"

"You took my baby. We know. They all knooooow, Paul," whispered Cynthia, a giant cockroach crawling out of her eye socket.

Paul turned and flew through the door into the bedroom. He ran to the bed, grabbed his head, and turned to look at the door, expecting the mother and daughter to follow.

"Ama! You promised!" he whispered.

As he sat watching the door, Paul's heart pounded. Suddenly a new truth was upon him, and it was one that he could barely accept. The spell Ama used to keep the spirits at bay was broken. Brenda and Cynthia's murdered faces proved as much. Had Ama's magic continued, Paul wouldn't be able to see the injuries the mother and daughter sustained at his hands. But now, he was able to see his cruel work in all its evil clarity; the crushed bone in the face of a mother, the little girl's blue curled lips and busted vessels in her small brown eyes as she sucked for air, the destroyed bond between mother and daughter – all at his hands.

Paul also realized that others would come for him. He and Ama had been thorough in their taking of life. All in all, they'd spilled the blood of over thirty people. And now Paul would be alone in receiving their wrath.

"Is this how it ends?" Paul asked while clutching the broken skull in his arms, clinging to hope that Ama would come to save him. But Ama didn't come. Instead, the murdered child and her mother continued speaking from the hallway.

"I was only a little girl when you took my mother away from me. Now I have no one. The grave is so cold. Every night I cry alone, shivering, with no one there to hold me."

"Paaaul.... Where is my Brenda? I can't find her. She's afraid of the dark, and she needs me. But you crushed my face, and now I can't see my baby. My eyes have fallen out. They're useless because of you. Who'll protect my little Brenda when the snakes come to eat her flesh? Will you help me find my baby?"

Suddenly Paul screamed.

"Amaaaaaa! Where are you?"

But the only sounds were those of a crying little girl just outside Paul's bedroom door.

Suddenly something hit the wall at the headboard of the bed. Paul jumped and moved to the center of the floor.

"I know you're in there, you sick son of a bitch!" said a man's voice.

Paul was about to leave the room when a young man walked through the wall behind him.

"You can't hide anymore, Paul. Everyone knows what you did."

Paul looked the boy over and didn't see any injuries that indicated he was one of his victims.

"Who are you? I don't remember you!"

"Really?"

The man lifted his head, and a large gash opened in his throat, shooting blood across the room. His eyes rolled back, and a gagging noise escaped the opening.

"Do you remember me now?"

Derrick. Paul did remember him. Ama had killed the man as he slept by running a blade across his throat.

"I....I didn't touch you!" explained Paul while backing away. "Ama did it."

The man moved closer to Paul.

"Do you think that absolves you of responsibility? You sell out! Enslaving your people for a woman that never loved you."

The words startled Paul, and he immediately went on the defensive.
"What? Ama loves me!"

"Really? Then where is she?"

"I...I don't know. Maybe something happened with that light."

The man lifted his head again, and blood sprayed through Paul. The man began speaking in a warbled voice through the gash in his neck.

"Go ahead. Tell yourself anything. But everyone knows you're a fool. Ama never loved you. She planned to take control of your people from the beginning, and you were the necessary fool."

"You're wrong! We've been together for years!"

"And how long do you think she's been practicing witchcraft?"

"I...I don't know. Only a few years."

"Ama has been studying the dark arts since she was a child. Through visions, she's been plotting this takeover of your people since she was a child in the Cherokee village. Why do you think they sent her to care for you when she was so young? Why do you think the Cherokee people so easily agreed to your marriage to Ama? They were happy to be rid of her evil, her poison."

"No!"

"She couldn't stop Mr. Green because she wanted to become Mr. Green!"

Paul began trembling uncontrollably. He didn't want to believe what the man was saying, but inside he'd always felt a bit – used by Ama. The way she'd mention something in passing and the way he'd always do what was requested. The way she'd mentioned killing the sharecroppers as a way to blunt Mr. Green's attack, that had all been her idea. Paul went along with it. A reasonable person would've never done such a thing. Paul didn't understand why he could never say no to Ama – until now.

While the victims of their horrific deeds surrounded him, Ama's absence made that "used" feeling all the more potent in the middle of this hell. He remembered all the times she was alone in their house while working in the fields. Sometimes when he came home, her behavior would be distant and dark, preoccupied with things that didn't seem attached to their married life. There were times when Ama seemed like someone else entirely.

"I don't believe you," Paul finally exclaimed after a moment of silence.

But the sound of his voice was so unconvincing that Paul didn't bother repeating it. His thoughts were of his wife, Ama, and deception.

"Yes. Search your feelings. You know what I'm saying is true. Ama used you to kill us."

Paul remembered the look on Ama's face when she took the life of her first victim. It was a cold blank look that rattled Paul to his core. There was no emotion. She moved from one victim to the next, like numbers on a list, only in a systematic manner.

"What do you want from me?" Paul finally asked. He was tired of the torture and wanted it to end.

The man turned and left the room.

"Hey! What do you want?" Paul screamed.

But the man was gone.

8:00 am:

Although he'd heard no disturbances since being confronted by the trio of victims he'd killed, Paul decided to stay holed up in the bedroom. Fear gripped him fiercely, and he didn't dare to face any more of the souls he and his wife had stolen. But that wasn't all.

Paul's heart lay broken into a thousand pieces. The sun was rising in the sky, and still, there was no Ama. Paul's eyes had been bewitched by Ama once more, fooled into believing that he saw what never occurred; the exploding of his wife's head as the light shot from the sky was all just a scheme to keep him in the dark while the beautiful liar made a stealthy getaway. And now Paul was left to pay the ultimate price.

As he stood hovering in the center of the room, Paul fantasized about all the ways the sharecroppers would seek their revenge.

"Maybe there are one or two witches among the group," he mumbled, fumbling with his skull, trying to break it into a thousand pieces. Maybe there was a hell and fucking over the deceased was the way to gain license there. Perhaps they would somehow reach out to Mr. Green.

"I'm sure he's itching for revenge."

Suddenly Paul sent the skull flying in the air, smashing it against the wall and shattering it into a thousand pieces. As he lowered his hand, the light of his tarnished wedding band caught his eye.

"Piece of shit isn't even gold," he murmured while holding the ring made of iron up for inspection.

"There's nothing they could ever do that is worse than what you've done," Paul whispered. He considered Ama's betrayal more destructive than any punishment he could receive, and it drove a rusty spike through his heart.

12:00 pm:

Filled with a sense of loneliness that he'd never felt before, Paul sat in the middle of the floor, brooding over his predicament.

"I wish they'd come and finish it already," he said while staring at the door. He knew all the people he'd killed were coming for him. He just didn't know how they'd get their revenge.

As he eyed the scattered bone of his skull on the floor, Paul noticed a larger piece of bone was slowly shaking back and forth. He watched it curiously, expecting a roach or a spider to crawl out from underneath. Instead, a piece of floorboard buckled and, all at once, pushed several pieces of bone aside.

"You're coming," Paul whispered, readying himself for his final departure.

Soon the floor began buckling in other parts of the room. Paul raised himself to float slightly above the floor as he watched all the floorboards bend upward, displacing whatever was sitting on them.

"I know you're here!" Paul yelled, wiping at his brow. Suddenly he froze and looked down at his palm. There was sweat!

"How is this possible?" he asked. The dead felt nothing. Paul hadn't felt anything other than emotion for years. It was one of the benefits of being dead - if there was a benefit. No feeling. Those were the rules, and he didn't make them. The one who wrote the beginning and end of every story did. And yet, here he was – perspiring, watching in disbelief as the rules to which everyone was supposed to adhere were broken.

It was within that moment that Paul realized the temperature in the room. It was hot! Hotter than anything Paul experienced in his living existence. He could see the heat waves distorting his vision as the temperature climbed.

"What devilment is this?" Paul asked aloud.

He could feel the sweat dripping down his back now, wetting underwear he hadn't changed for years. Paul reached up and scratched at his underarms, remembering that he only did so when he became afraid.

"Come get me!" he yelled, pretending to be happy to have it all end. But he was displeased, and all he could think of was how Ama had masterminded such a horrific ending for the man she pretended to love.

Soon creaking sounds rang out; the whole house was reacting to the heat, twisting and bending itself, unable to withstand the intense unexplained change.

Suddenly the door burst into flames.

Paul flew backward. He could feel the intense heat radiating throughout the room, and it hurt his skin. Paul lifted his hand to his face in astonishment.

"It hurts."

Finally, the whole house exploded, sending Paul sailing through the air.

12:05 pm:

When Paul opened his eyes, he was lying face down on the grass in front of the house. Blood poured from his mouth, and his head was throbbing. He tried to lift himself from the ground but fell flat on his face; the pain from his injuries was too great. Paul had awkwardly landed on both his arms, breaking them both; one of his forearms had a bone sticking out of his skin, while the other arm felt limp and rattled like gravel was inside.

"Am I alive?" Paul groaned. "What's going on?"

Paul noticed that pain shot through his face and down his neck when he opened his mouth. He could tell there were burns over most of his body.

"Ama! Help! Somebody!" he yelled out.

More than help, Paul wanted an explanation of what had happened to him. The events were beyond his understanding. Dead people weren't supposed to bleed or feel pain. Was he alive? Had he been dreaming of his death? His marriage to Ama, had it all been one big fantasy? Paul didn't care if one of the ghosts came to him. He wanted an answer to this confusing mess.

Suddenly a ray of light hit Paul on the left side of his face, making him slide across the grass.

"Shiiiit!" he screamed out as his broken bones shifted underneath his skin.

Paul rolled over to try to see what had hit him, but another blast hit him in the face. This time the rays hit Paul in his eyes, causing his whole head to glow a strange red. Suddenly his head burst into flame.

"AAAAHHHH!" he yelled. "Somebody! Help me!"

Paul squeezed his eyes shut and swatted at his face. Although his eyes were closed, Paul started seeing strange colors flashing inside his head like sparkles. He could smell the odor of his flesh burning in the heat of the light, sizzling as blisters rose on his face, his eyelids, his lips.

"I'm blind! I'm fucking blind!" Paul yelled out.

And then Paul noticed something strange.

There was no new pain aside from the injuries he'd sustained in the initial house fire. Although the fire was burning his skin, it didn't hurt him.

Paul crawled to his knees, grabbed a handful of grass, and rubbed it all over his face. After extinguishing the fire, he stood and cautiously opened his eyes. He reached up and gently touched his eyelids. Although the fire had lit on them, his eyes were okay, and the strange colors were gone. After surveying his body for additional injuries, Paul sat on the ground and began sobbing.

"I don't understand," he sobbed. "What's happening to me?"

Through his tears, Paul noticed movement close to the forest. The sharecroppers were there, and none of them were paying attention to the injured murderer. Instead, they all stood gazing in awe at something – a strange thin creature surrounded by light.

"I've got to get out of here," said Paul. He tried to fly away and was unable to.

"Damn it! Move!" he barked to himself as he pushed from within, trying to fly away. Still, he was unable to leave. Paul stomped the ground in frustration and immediately regretted doing so; blood was pouring from the open wounds on his arms.

"I don't get it," he growled.

Paul tore a piece of his shirt and made a tourniquet for his arm.

"Dead people aren't supposed to feel pain," he grumbled, wincing as he applied pressure to the wound. Comfortable that the injuries could withstand movement, Paul began walking towards the group.

As he drew closer, Paul started to hear strange whisperings in his head; a voice that was unintended for his audience yet loud enough for all to listen.

"The spell is gone," the voice whispered. "Let all who has suffered breathe the clean air of freedom." Paul struggled to see the visitor's face, but he could not do so. The whispering in his head sounded so much like – home.

Suddenly a stiff gust of wind began blowing that caused Paul to step back in surprise with his mouth ajar. Paul closed his eyes and allowed the air to cool his burning skin. Intrigued, Paul decided to move closer to get a better look.

Although the creature wore a long hooded robe made of light, Paul could tell the visitor was female; its body swayed back and forth in the wind with an almost hypnotic, feminine rhythm. But the being didn't have a face. Instead, in the center of the hood was a silvery fluid, like water, reflecting whoever was closest to it.

The being was much taller than Paul expected too. Although it stood in one place, it seemed to drift back and forth as if pulled by invisible strings.

As he walked towards the group, Paul began to get nervous. What if the mob attacked him? What if they all remembered what he'd done? Still, Paul couldn't help himself. He had to know what was going on. He, too, was drawn to the creature at the edge of the forest.

As Paul moved closer, he heard the whispers of the sharecroppers.

"Who's next?"

"Shall he go?"

"What about you?"

"Shall we go together?"

"The children!"

"Yes, the children! Let the youth show us the way!"

"The babies have suffered the most, and they deserve peace."

The was bustling, and then four frightened children appeared in front of the group.

"Don't be afraid," a familiar voice said. Paul saw Cynthia, the woman who had tormented him in the house, push Brenda to the front of the group. Their horrifying appearances were gone.

"I'll be right behind you," Cynthia whispered, leading her daughter to the creature.

Suddenly the creature opened its arms to the children, and a golden light shot out from its chest. But unlike the horrific injuries inflicted upon Paul's flesh, the light had a different effect on the children's skin. The light seemed to rejuvenate their appearances, making them seem more beautiful.

"You are free," the creature whispered.

Reluctantly, the children walked into the light. As the golden brilliance absorbed them, Paul could hear the children's laughter floating on the wind. Suddenly, the light stopped shining, and the children were gone.

Paul continued watching. One by one, each of the sharecroppers walked to the creature, was bathed in golden light, and disappeared. Paul heard each sharecropper's joyous song of freedom ring out in the wind after they passed, happiness so pure that most of them laughed and cried at once.

Paul could do nothing but watch from a distance, reminded of the damage he'd caused, feeling helplessly ashamed.

"Fucking Ama," he said under his breath. Shame was such a heavy burden to carry alone. Although the sun was shining and the spirits of his victims found their way to paradise, Paul was acutely aware of the absence of freedom in his own life. Much like the souls Ama trapped, he, too, felt shackled in chains by Ama's deceit.

Finally, when the last victim walked into the light, and the final burst of laughter tickled the leaves on the edge of the forest, Paul stood alone with the creature. They both stared at one another, yet only one of them was broken.

Paul stumbled over to the creature and stood in front of it. Racked with fear, he was unable to find his tongue. He just stood there staring, longing for freedom.

The creature didn't speak. Its thin body just hovered, watching the pitiful man beg silently for something his sins couldn't provide.

After a while, Paul grew frustrated with the creature's posturing and decided to ask outright for what he wanted.

"What about me? Can I go too?"

The creature drifted back slightly before responding.

"Yoooou?" It asked incredulously. "What makes you think you are worthy of such a gift?"

The creature leaned down from high up in the air, its torso bending in two like an enormous stick of licorice. There was a splash, and slowly, the silvery liquid drained off the creature's face to reveal a human face underneath – it was Imani! Paul's body went limp with fear as the woman's face moved closer to his.

"You and I have never had the pleasure. I am Imani."

"Who?"

"You were supposed to meet me when you died. But your wife interfered."

Once again, Paul's heart jumped at the mention of his wife.

"Ama! Do you know where she is?"

"She is not dead."

"Where is she? Can you take me to her?"

"The two of you will see each other soon enough."

Paul looked confused.

"What does that mean?"

"Your flesh has been restored, has it not?"

"Yes, but I don't understand why. Dead people don't...."

"You've enslaved spirits. Let me tell you. There isn't a crime worse than what you've done. You will pay penitence through the sufferings of the living; you will feel pain and emotion just as the living does. But you will be unable to die."

"You mean the sharecroppers. I know. It was never my intention to...."

Imani held up her long hand to stop Paul's explanation.

"I am neither judge nor jury. I am only a shepherd of souls, a deity ensuring the safe transition from the living into the hereafter."

"But I'm just trying to explain."

Imani gave Paul a warm smile.

"In time, it is possible for you to gain entrance into the hereafter. But until you repay the debt, you are in exile."

"Exile? What does that mean? How long do I have to wait?"

Imani closed her eyes and leaned back. Suddenly, the mercury-like substance began rushing in from both sides of the robe. Imani thrashed her head back and forth, fighting the submersion as it poured into her eyes, nose, and mouth. When the process finished, Imani's face was gone, and only the reflective liquid remained.

"Imani! Will you talk to me? What am I supposed to do?" asked Paul.

A gargling metallic noise sounded from deep inside Imani's robe. Her tall body began growing whiter and whiter, smelling of cinnamon as it burned. Soon her long thin arms separated from her body fell to the ground, and dissolved. The remaining body shook violently. A loud popping noise sounded until the head separated from the torso and slammed into the ground. The rest of her body burned brighter and brighter. Finally, it exploded, sending rays of light shooting into the sky.

Shaken by what he'd witnessed, Paul walked over to look at Imani's liquid-filled head. Frustrated, he kicked it and covered the tip of his shoes in the thick gooey substance.

"What the hell am I supposed to do now?" he asked. The substance drained out of the head to show Imani's bloodless face. Suddenly she opened her eyes.

"Survive," Imani said softly. Her head exploded and melted into the ground.

Paul stared at the pile of flesh as it disintegrated.

"Survive?" he asked, feeling more confused.

A noise sounded to Paul's right, and he turned to look. Several giant oak trees began shaking violently, like someone – or something was moving them. Next, the ground started rumbling. Paul struggled to maintain his balance as the ground beneath him shook like an earthquake, forcing him to the ground. Paul looked up at the trees.

"Survive," Paul mouthed, his eyes glued to the swaying trees. He could hear something pushing through the forest towards him. There seemed to be an army of monsters. Hundreds of demons, maybe thousands. The sounds were pouring out of the woods like a nightmare.

The whispering, growling and screaming - all on a direct path to Paul's location.

Paul slowly backed away.

"I've got to get out of here."

Paul knew what was coming. Ama's spell was gone. The demons she'd kept off the land were free and could invade at any moment. Unlike previous events, they were coming for Paul, and no magic could protect him.

Paul turned and started running towards the burning house. Just as he did, a wolflike beast the size of a horse burst from the forest. The creature's eyes locked on Paul, and it released a blood-chilling howl. Seeing the monster gave wings to Paul's feet, and he sprinted faster as the beast gave chase.

"Jesus Christ!" Paul screamed.

Another creature emerged from the forest as he ran past the burning house. This time it was a demon with red skin and massive horns. In its hand were hundreds of long squirming white worms and a bow. The monster saw Paul and dropped the worms in a pile, all squealing and biting at one another. The demon grabbed one of the worms and ran the slimy creature across his tongue. The worm became as straight and stiff as an arrow.

"We know who you are!" the demon hissed as it aimed at Paul.

The demon placed the frozen worm into the bow, aimed at Paul, and let the arrow fly. Paul stopped running, and the demonic projectile missed and landed in the soil at Paul's feet. Grateful for the demon's poor aim, Paul smirked at the monster before attempting to escape. But as he turned to flee, he tripped and fell to the ground. Worms were all over Paul's legs. This time it was the demon's turn to smile; he'd intentionally missed Paul instead choosing the soil at his feet. The worm spawned hundreds of hungry white worms, and they all attacked Paul, biting him with their sharp teeth.

"AAAHHHHH!" a horrified Paul screamed.

Paul could feel a few of the slimy demonic worms inside his legs. They'd created wounds and gotten beneath his skin, eating and crawling up towards his groin. He lept to his feet and tried brushing off as many animals as he could. He slapped at his genitals, trying to smash the monsters before they crawled higher.

But suddenly, there was another disturbance from the forest. Hundreds of ghosts poured out onto the property, all frightful spirits from hell.

"He wants you!" The leader of the ghosts yelled. "Take him!"

The army of undead sprinted towards Paul, all of them screaming and falling over one another as they pursued him.

"No....no....no," yelled Paul, pushing himself to run on.

As he tore through the bushes, he could feel the monsters' footsteps pounding the ground in pursuit. He had to make it to Ama's well in the weeds. It was the only place he had left to go.

15

Son of the Buffalo

Wilson was sleeping when he heard an annoying noise rattling in the background. He mumbled incoherently and turned on his side to continue his slumber. But the buzzing noise in his head wouldn't go away, and it grew louder. Eventually, Wilson figured out that the sound was a voice – one that he'd heard before. Soon additional sounds of other people talking invaded Wilson's place of rest.

"Is he breathing?"

"Shake him. That ought to wake him up."

"Wilson!"

The voices grew louder. Closer. Soon the talking was a blaring noise that wouldn't go away. Slowly, Wilson began to move.

"Uggggh," he groaned.

"He's waking up," the voice continued. "Hey, Wilson!"

Wilson began blinking his eyes. Through blurry vision, he saw a familiar face looming over him.

"What's going on? Five more minutes," he mumbled.

"That's it, bro. Time to wake up," the voice continued.

"Shut the hell up, Michael. You're so annoying sometimes," protested Wilson.

The name jogged Wilson's memory, and he jumped to his feet.

"Michael!"

"Yes, it's me."

Wilson embraced his little brother in a giant hug.

"I thought you were dead."

Michael wrapped his arms around Wilson's waist and squeezed his brother tight.

"I thought you were dead too. What happened?"

Wilson's eyes eventually fell on Takatoka and Tariq. Both the boys looked like they'd been through a war.

"Guys! What happened?"

"We don't know. We were all knocked out."

Wilson looked around. It was night, and they were still at the clearing in the forest. Wilson looked up into the sky and noticed that the eclipse was still there. It had the same strange markings on it, and it continued bathing everything in the same disgusting red light. Soon the other boys also began staring at the peculiar moon.

"How is the eclipse still here?" asked Wilson.

"Yeah, we don't know either. We were out for a few hours. How is the eclipse still happening?" asked Tariq.

Wilson didn't have any answers. His head was still thick with the fog of sleep. He rubbed his eyes, trying to wake up.

"And then there's that," said Takatoka pointing towards the far end of the field. Wilson turned to look.

Planted at the edge of the clearing were three towering sequoia trees. Encased in the center of each enormous tree trunk were three people - Nana Ama, Grandma Noya, and a strange-looking man.

"Grandma Noya!"

Wilson ran over to the trees.

"I don't understand. Were these here before?" Wilson asked.

"They must've shown up when everyone got knocked out. I don't remember seeing these two big trees, and I don't remember Grandma Noya being here," replied Michael.

Wilson began to shiver as he looked at his grandmother. Her body stood frozen in a thick brown substance resembling tree sap. The expression on her face was more frightening than anything Wilson had ever seen; her face was contorted with her lower jaw askew like she had been attempting to speak when something broke her jaw. She stared at the boys with wide, teary eyes filled with terror.

Lying next to Grandma Noya was Wilson's great-grandmother Ama. A wound ran down the crown of her head that parted her skull like a loaf of bread. Wilson gagged a little when he saw her brain protruding, a pink frost glistening on top of it. Her face, too, was frozen; her eyes were squeezed shut, and her mouth was open like she had been screaming when her injuries happened.

The other boys walked over to Wilson and stared at the bodies.

"I thought they were dead," whispered Michael.

"Me too," replied Wilson.

Wilson moved closer and lifted a finger to touch his grandmother. Takatoka pulled his arm away.

"I wouldn't do that if I were you. What if it captures you?"

Wilson lowered his hand, and Michael quickly latched onto it as the two boys stared at their grandmother.

Wilson moved to the last body – the man who had been in his dreams. It was Mr. Green. Unlike the others, there was no look of pain or anger on his face. There were severe burns on his hands, yet his expression was a stoic one. He didn't display emotion. Instead, he stared straight ahead as if he were looking directly into Wilson's eyes.

Michael squeezed Wilson's hand as they stared at the man.

"That's the man that tortured me," he whispered.

Wilson bit his lip in anger.

"Asshole!" he whispered between clenched teeth. "What did he do to you?"

Michael ignored the question and stared at the ground in silence. Soon tears began trickling down his face. Wilson wrapped his arm around his brother's shoulders, and the two boys watched their grandmother in silence.

Suddenly Grandma Noya began convulsing.

"Holy shit!" exclaimed Michael as both brothers fell to the ground. The other two boys quickly retreated to the edge of the woods.

"She's alive!"

Wilson jumped up and ran to Grandma Noya.

"Grandma Noya! Can you hear me?"

The old woman's eyes locked on Wilson. She tried to tell him something but could not move her mouth. Finally, her body convulsed a few more times, and then she stopped moving.

"Help me get her out of there!" yelled Wilson. "Get something to break her out!"

Wilson and Michael searched the ground looking for something strong enough to break through the encasements. Nervously, both Takatoka and Tariq moved away from them.

"Dude, I know she's your grandmother, but I wouldn't fuck with those trees. Something had to put them inside. Touching those things might get us all killed," warned Tariq.

Wilson stopped searching and turned to Tariq.

"What do you expect me to do, just leave her there? That's my grandmother stuck in that tomb!"

"I know, but there are other questions that need answering."

"Like what?"

"Didn't you say your grandmother and great-grandmother died?"

"Yeah. Maybe Mr. Green brought them back for some twisted purpose."

Tariq shook his head.

"Just think about what you said for a minute. It doesn't make sense."

"Maybe if it were your family under that asshole's control, you'd be able to see my point of view."

"Come on, man. Think about it. Mr. Green, the most racist motherfucker on earth, suddenly decides to bring both your *Cherokee* relatives back to life? Why? Because he was lonely? Not a fucking chance. Not only that, Mr. Green places them in a weird cryogenic freezer, along with himself no less, and waits for someone to come along and find them? Does that sound believable to you? Not me. There's something strange going on in your family. You're just too pussy to admit it."

Wilson glared at Tariq. He wanted to fight him, but he knew Tariq wasn't the real problem. Something about the boy's words made sense.

Wilson felt Michael tugging on his arm.

"He's right, bro. Something's not right."

Frustrated, Wilson snapped at his little brother.

"Like what?"

"Like maybe our whole family has been lying to us from the beginning. Mom and Dad know more than what they've told us. And seeing as how Grandma Noya kept the secret about your powers away from us for so long, maybe both Grandma Noya and Nana Ama are at the center of this mess. I could be wrong, but I doubt it. Something sure stinks like shit."

Wilson tried not to laugh, but he couldn't help it. Michael was a foul-mouthed old man stuffed inside the body of a child. He'd missed Michael's cursing. The kid had a be-damned way of saying what was on his mind, regardless of the audience. And he was usually right. As much as he hated to admit it, Michael was right. Something wasn't adding up.

Tariq began laughing.

"What so funny?" asked Michael.

"You two," replied Tariq. "You guys don't even knooooooooo....."

Tariq's mouth froze. Soon a dazed look appeared on his face. He began trembling, and white foam started pouring from his mouth. His body whole body locked, and he fell. Before Tariq landed on his face, Takatoka grabbed his friend's shirt and lowered him to the ground.

"Tariq! What is it?" asked Takatoka.

Wilson ran to the boy's side.

"What's wrong with him?" he asked.

"I don't know. It might be...."

Slowly, both Takatoka and Wilson stood and looked around the edge of the clearing. Although the eclipse illuminated everything in red light, the boys struggled to see.

"I can't see anything."

"Me either."

Suddenly an idea came to Wilson. He reached up to touch his eyelid. Just as he was about to activate his powers, Michael stopped him.

"Wilson! Don't! You're going to get us killed!"

Wilson looked over at his brother. Michael was nervously peeling the skin from his lips and whining softly. Wilson was touched to see the emotion exhibited by his kid brother. Michael usually hid everything behind a veil of anger, but this time was different. Michael was crying.

"Let's get out of here," Michael complained through bloody lips. "I don't like this."

Wilson looked at his brother and felt anger once more. Mr. Green's torturing of Michael had done something to the child. Wilson could see that the boy wasn't himself, and Michael was – affected.

"We can't just leave him here, Mike. He risked his life to help me find you."

Michael looked down at Tariq and started crying harder.

"I just want to get out of here! Something's coming!"

"Ooooooooo..." Tariq continued, unable to complete the sentence or stop the unfinished word's long pronunciation.

Suddenly there was a loud popping noise, and both Tariq's upper body and lower body rose on a slant as if something were bending him in two. Both Wilson and Takatoka jumped out of the way.

"What's happening?" asked Takatoka.

"I don't know!" replied Wilson. "I don't know!"

Soon Tariq's waistline was buried in the dirt, his legs pressed against the back of his head like a pocket knife as he sunk more and more. His drawn-out word changed to blood-filled gurgles as blood poured from his mouth and his eyes.

"Wilson....ggggg....help me!"

But Wilson could do nothing but watch as the excruciating torture of his friend became more brutal. Soon Tariq was buried chest-deep in the soil with his face covered in a thick sludge of blood and dirt. All he could do was take small inhalations without breathing out.

"Help! Aggggg…" he begged as the pain overwhelmed him.

"Tariq!" Takatoka cried.

Wilson couldn't ignore his powers any longer. He touched his eyelid and looked around the clearing. Wilson gasped at what he saw. There were thousands of ghosts surrounding them - spirits that were not human. They were buffaloes.

"Oh my God!" whispered Wilson.

"What is it?" asked Takatoka.

Wilson continued staring at the thousands of ghostly buffaloes surrounding them. There were so many of the creatures. They all seemed agitated, pushing and jostling with one another for the best position to storm the field while thick saliva fell from their jowls. Their heavy and labored breathing cast a giant cloud of fog over most of the buffaloes, partially obscuring them from view. A few of the creatures bellowed and sent the others into a collective frenzy; the animals kicked and screamed like angry bulls teased to the point of explosion. But in a second or two, the beasts calmed. Wilson could tell that something was holding them back.

"What is it, Wilson?" asked Takatoka.

Wilson could feel their anger radiating through the forest; the buffaloes' hatred for the boys was so intense that he was sweating.

Wilson quickly deactivated his power.

"We've….got to help Tariq," he finally said.

Wilson ran to Michael. He pulled the boy close.

"Mike," he whispered. "It's okay. We have to be calm."

But Michael couldn't stop crying. He melted in his brother's arms and started sobbing uncontrollably as soon as he saw the fear in Wilson's eyes.

"We're going to die now, aren't we?"

Wilson hugged his brother tighter and leaned down to whisper in his ear.

"Not if you do as I say. Do you still have the triangle?"

Michael never heard the question. He was too preoccupied with death.

"Will we see one another in heaven? What if we can't find each other? What if I go to hell and you go to...."

"Focus, Mike! Do you still have the triangle?"

"Yeah. It's in my pocket."

Takatoka stood up.

"Maybe you should think about teleporting us all out of here."

"I can't just leave my relatives here to die."

"I'm not saying you have to leave them permanently. Maybe we can come back later. But if we don't get out of here now, we won't make it out alive."

Wilson turned to look at his brother. After seeing the fear in Michael's eyes, he turned to Takatoka.

"Okay. Let's go. You grab Tariq."

Takatoka took one step towards Tariq and froze.

"Hey! Takatoka, you okay?" asked Wilson.

Takatoka took one more step and fell to the ground, landing on his face.

"Takatoka!" yelled Wilson. He ran over and knelt beside the boy.

"They're dead!" screamed Michael. "They're all dead!"

Wilson ignored his little brother and tried to roll Takatoka over onto his back.

"Come on, Takatoka."

He grabbed the boy's jacket and tried to move him, but he couldn't.

"You okay, dude?" he asked, struggling once more to turn his friend over.

Suddenly Takatoka's jacket ripped open to expose his back. Wilson ran to Michael and tried to turn him away from what was happening, but he couldn't – Michael was too afraid, paralyzed by fear. Together the two brothers watched in horror as an invisible force ripped the skin off Takatoka's back like a sheet of paper, sending blood everywhere.

"I can't take this anymore, " cried Michael. "Get us out of here, Wilson."

Wilson closed his eyes and pushed down in the center of his body. But nothing happened. He closed his eyes again and concentrated harder. Still, they didn't transport.

Suddenly Takatoka's eyes opened. He looked around for a few seconds, and then the pain hit him.

"AHHHHHH!" he screamed. "GET ME OUT OF HERE!"

Suddenly his body began rising and falling back to the ground – higher and harder like someone was pounding the boy into the ground.

"MOMMY!" Takatoka screamed, his mouth filling with blood.

Soon the pain was too great for him to bear, and Takatoka fell unconscious again.

"Is he dead?" asked Michael.

Wilson let go of his brother and moved closer to look at his friend – Takatoka was still alive, but he was having difficulty breathing. Wilson extended his hand towards the boy.

"Takatoka?"

Suddenly Takatoka's head slammed hard against the ground. Something cut into the child's skin, creating a large incision stretching from the back of his neck down to his waist.

Horrified, Wilson tapped his eyelid to activate his powers.

"Where are you, you son of a bitch?" he yelled while spinning.

But nothing happened. Wilson's powers didn't activate, so he began slapping at his eye frantically.

"Come on....come on...." He yelled continuously—still, no powers.

Takatoka's body jerked once more before his head raised off the ground. A tremendous amount of blood poured from his mouth as his eyes opened slightly.

"Wilson....what's happening?" Takatoka asked, both of his eyes swollen.

"Just close your eyes, Takatoka. It'll all be over soon," replied Wilson.

Suddenly, Takatoka's head slammed into the ground with such force that blood sprayed everywhere, drenching both Wilson and Michael.

Michael buried his face in Wilson's chest.

"I want to go home," he cried.

There was a loud cracking noise, and Takatoka's spine exited his body through the incision on his back, completely emptying the rest of the boy's blood on the forest floor. His spinal cord rose a few feet above his pale, lifeless body and began hovering. Soon it burst into flame.

Suddenly a deep voice echoed through the forest.

"We despise you."

Wilson frantically searched the forest. Although the buffaloes were ghosts, he expected to see them pouring out to attack him at any moment. But he saw nothing.

"I know you're there! I can feel it!" he whispered.

Unable to see anything, he tapped his eye once again, only to discover his powers still didn't work.

"Shit!" he cursed in frustration.

"We hate everything about you," the voice continued. "The way you eat, the way you talk, your laughter – everything about your kind is a putrid song worthy of death."

Something moved in Wilson's peripheral vision, and he turned to look. Walking out of the shadows at the far end of the clearing was one lone buffalo, a small brown animal with an enormous horned head. It limped as it walked towards the boys. Its feet made a clicking sound as it walked, making it sound like the animal was walking on a wooden floor. Stuck deep in the head of the buffalo was a hatchet. The injury it made seemed to be bleeding, making the buffalo shake its head occasionally to toss away the blood.

"What's that?" whispered Michael.

"Grandma Noya would call that a Tatanka, I think," responded Wilson.

"A Tatanka? You mean a buffalo?" asked Michael.

"Yeah," answered Wilson.

Michael clutched Wilson tighter.

"Is it going to kill us?"

"I don't know."

Suddenly the Buffalo's voice thundered across the clearing.

"Silence, you sniveling imbeciles. The ground you stand upon is a sacred cemetery. Beneath this molded soil lies the souls of our ancestors - the ones your kind extinguished so callously. It would be an honor for my ancestors to see your death! We should spill your blood today in celebration."

When the buffalo reached the center of the field, it stopped. Its lips didn't move, but the animal's voice echoed throughout the forest.

"We have waited for hundreds of years, but now the moment is upon us. The light of Oshua's Red Moon shines, and we will take back what is ours!"

The trees all around the field started trembling. Soon Wilson could feel the thunderous hooves of all the buffalo running out of the forest – but he couldn't see them. They were ghosts and were invisible with normal eyes.

"Ow!" Wilson suddenly cried out. He grabbed his side and doubled over in pain. Michael knelt beside Wilson.

"Wilson! What is it?"

"Nothing."

Wilson raised his hand and saw blood on his palm. Michael's eyes widened.

"How did that happen?"

"I don't know. I was just...."

Wilson felt another sharp pain in the small of his back this time. His legs went numb, and he tumbled to the ground. Michael was furious.

"You fucking asshole son of a bitches! He's just a kid! Show yourselves, you pussies!"

Suddenly Michael screamed.

"OW! AHHHHH..."

He dropped to his knees beside Wilson and grabbed his legs. There were two deep punctures in the back of both his thighs.

"You will silence yourselves in the presence of Jericho! This world is not yours. You are unwelcome invaders, a disease infecting this land. You are thieves, and we will have what you have taken, one way or another."

Wilson looked over at his little brother bleeding on the ground, and he could no longer contain his rage.

"Who are you, and why are you doing this to us? We're only kids!"

The buffalo laughed.

"Children? Babies? Are those your terms of engagement for the world? Let us see the truth within your lies ."

Wilson and Michael watched silently as the ghostly figures of soldiers ran onto the clearing. Just as the recording had played for Michael, it replayed for Wilson. But this time, Wilson and Michael were not in the images. Instead, there were the original Buffaloes.

"I saw this," whispered Michael.

Wilson watched the images in silence. Although he was frightened, he began to understand the creatures' pain. He remembered the stories his Grandmother Noya told him about the Native American plight - how the U.S. Government tried to kill them by attacking their primary food source, the buffalo. When all was said and done, the government campaign proved to be a murderous success; they slaughtered millions of buffalo and nearly wiped both the Native Americans and the buffalo from the face of the earth.

After remembering what his grandmother had told him, Wilson decided to speak up.

"My people are both Cherokee and African. We are not your enemy. We are both victims of the same evil. My people have died under the same blade that killed your relatives. We are brothers in pain."

Jericho lifted his head and stared directly into Wilson's eyes. Suddenly Wilson doubled over in pain.

"Do not equate your pitiful lives with ours! We are not the same! The indigenous man has killed my relatives for years. How dare you try to ignore your crimes."

"But we only killed for survival, and we never intended to kill without purpose. The government used you to try and kill my people."

"Even your statement of innocence stinks of evil. Your reason for killing our brothers and sisters is irrelevant. It only matters that our tribe is lighter by your need, your never-ending arrogance."

Wilson quickly turned to look at Mr. Green inside the tree.

"This man that you have captured belongs to the same tribe that attacked your relatives and mine. Mr. Green is a vile racist who wants nothing but to murder."

"We do not assign guilt based upon the color of skin. To us, humans all possess one trait – the desire to destroy. You are human and therefore responsible for the depletion of our bloodline, and you all shall pay the price."

Michael moaned and climbed to his feet. Wilson tried pulling his brother to the ground.

"Michael!" Wilson whispered. "No!"

Michael ignored his brother and spoke.

"It's you that's being arrogant, not us. We didn't try to hurt you - we don't even know you. But here you are torturing us. You're not even listening, even though what Wilson says is the truth. Stop being a dickhead and listen to my brother."

Jericho lowered his head to the ground.

"Michael! Get down!"

"Fuck him! He's going to kill us because he wants revenge? We didn't do anything!"

Jericho lifted his head and slammed into the dirt. This time the hatchet in his head began glowing. There was a short delay then the weapon shot a spark into the ground.

"Run!" screamed Wilson.

Michael tried to run, but he could barely move because of the holes in his legs. He took several steps and fell onto his stomach.

"Michael!" Wilson screamed.

But it was too late. A bolt of lightning zigzagged through the ground until it reached the boy. It shot into his legs and lifted him off the ground, where he remained suspended, convulsing from the electric shock.

"Let go of my brother!" yelled Wilson with tears streaming down his face. But there was only laughter from Jericho as Michael shook, continuously electrified.

Wilson stared at his brother through tears and felt sadness in his heart. Michael was just a kid, and he didn't deserve to pay for the sins of others.

As the boy continued receiving bursts of electricity, his body began to fade away. Soon Wilson could see Michael's organs; his heart, his lungs, his liver – all became visible while his body diminished. Soon Michael's outer body was solid glass while the organs inside his body remained flesh.

"We could take his life any time we feel like it."

Wilson stopped crying and stared at Jericho.

"You want something."

Jericho laughed again.

"This is why we chose you. Although we despise you, your intelligence grows by the hour."

Annoyed by the compliment, Wilson glared at the animal.

"Just tell me what the hell you want."

Jericho took a few more steps towards Wilson, his hoofs clicking on the soil as he moved.

"You will be the one to rid this place of humans."

Wilson didn't speak. Instead, he stared at Jericho, hating him for what he was doing to Michael.

"The power of Oshua's Red Moon only occurs every thousand years. There are endless possibilities to those with the skill to unlock its secrets. We unlocked Oshua's secrets, and through that power, we will use you as a weapon."

"You plan to use me to kill all humans on earth?"

"Fool, we are not like you, simple-minded humans! We are not preoccupied with power. We only want what is ours – this land."

"But why me?"

"We selected you before you were born. By studying the many cycles of the moons, we found you. You're the perfect weapon against a soulless enemy. Your arrival signals certain death for the humans!"

The ground began rumbling as the ghosts of the Buffaloes stamped their feet in celebration, sending Wilson sliding across the grass. After they calmed and Wilson righted himself, Jericho continued speaking.

"In the universe, all things are possible. The signs told us of a mixed-blood child that would lead us out of the darkness; that child would wield the powers of dark magic and use that power to rid us of our enemy."

"How am I supposed to do that?"

"You are human, so your nature is destruction. There are endless possibilities."

"If you're so powerful, why don't you do it yourself?"

"This place is our land, our home. Our preference is peaceful removal, violent extermination if necessary—our species is one of peace. Mass murder is not our original choice. This man, Mr. Green, belongs to you – the humans. If we allow him to continue on his path of destruction, he will certainly destroy all living things in this world, us included. It is better if we use the power of Oshua's Red Moon to hold him captive, to provide you an opportunity to rid this land of humans without bringing unnecessary attention to our kind."

"Wait, you are using Mr. Green as a failsafe to destroy everyone?"

"Precisely. Oshua's Red Moon allows us to hold him for five years in an unconscious state, and his powers lie dormant."

"What happens during those five years?"

"We will use Oshua's Moon to reverse time, to take you back five years, essentially erasing all memory of Mr. Green's damage."

"You will reverse time? Really? What about my family?"

"Aside from the one you call Nana Ama, they will all reappear with their memories stripped."

"Why not her?"

"She seeks world domination through witchcraft. She is a threat to your mission."

"But my other family would be brought back? Michael and Grandma Noya too?"

"Yes."

"What about my friends?"

"Returned."

"Why would you bring them back?"

"Your comfort during this period is essential to the successful removal of the humans."

"You want me comfortable so that I can commit mass murder?"

"We did not say that you needed to murder them all. If there is a way for you to remove them through peaceful means, that is acceptable. Still, death will be inevitable to overcome certain obstacles. For us, we do not care if you kill all humans, but we partially accept your moral dilemma in the matter, as long as the mission is successful."

Wilson began running through various scenarios that could force people to move in mass.

"There is something else you must know."

"What?"

"To demonstrate your commitment to the primary objective, you will have one week to take the lives of five people."

"I thought you said I didn't have to kill."

"One person for every year Oshua's Red Moon holds Mr. Green in captivity, to remind you that you only have five years until we release him."

"And what if I don't do it?"

"We will use Oshua's Red Moon to take your family's lives and unleash Mr. Green upon the world. Through Mr. Green's release, everyone will die, including us, but your loss will be the greatest, knowing you had the opportunity to save your family and instead chose to be selfish."

Wilson looked at Mr. Green and rubbed his vein-covered cheek. Mr. Green's presence always triggered a deformity in his face, and Wilson didn't understand why. Finally, he turned his attention back to Jericho.

"What about all the creatures that piece of shit created in the forest? Did you get rid of those too?"

"You scum! Do you think we care about the human souls lost to the demons in the forest? Your people skinned my ancestors and ate our flesh while fashioning our crowns of majesty as weapons in your arrows and tools. You deserve nothing more than terror."

"Then what's the point of reversing time for five years? If you're going to allow those demons to roam around killing people, you may as well let Mr. Green out."

Jericho closed his eyes and bowed his head. A considerable amount of time passed as he sat in silence, thinking about what Wilson had said. Soon he raised his head to speak.

"Disgusting human! We will eliminate most of the creatures your evil brother Mr. Green created. But not all of them. Some of hell's offspring must be allowed to feast on human flesh."

"But doesn't that make the mission more difficult?"

"Perhaps. But granting license to a few of hell's creatures accomplishes two things – it avenges the deaths of some of our brothers and sisters while also reminding you to stay on mission. We can accept this small, marginally satisfying inconvenience to you."

Wilson looked at his brother Michael floating in the air.

"Wipe his memory," he said while nodding towards his brother. "I don't want him remembering the torture."

"Done."

Wilson turned to look at his Grandmother Noya encased in the tree.

"Wipe her memory too. She shouldn't have to remember Nana Ama this way."

Jericho laughed.

"Such a senseless waste of Oshua's power. It would be easier if we painted the forest with the blood of your two precious family members."

"If you kill my family, I won't help you."

"Do you think we need your help?"

"You need me to help you take back the place you call home. It's either that or let that asshole Mr. Green destroy everything. You decide."

Jericho sat staring at Wilson, shifting side to side as he marveled at the boy's courage. Finally, he spoke.

"Do you accept the mission?"

Wilson paused before finally responding.

"Okay. I'll do it."

Jericho quickly banged his head onto the ground three times, and a light flashed. Fear consumed Wilson once more as he saw all the buffaloes surrounding him materialize out of thin air. The two creatures closest to him rammed their horns into his stomach and lifted him high above their heads.

"You nasty human scum!" the buffalo said, twirling him above her head as Wilson cried out in pain.

"I agreed to take the mission! What are you doing?" Wilson screamed.

"Relax, silly human," another buffalo grumbled. "It is all a part of the process."

Soon everything started dimming. Wilson looked over at his little brother and saw his body beginning to return to its normal state. He heard Tariq scream out.

"Tariq!" Wilson yelled, beginning to blackout.

When he looked over at Grandma Noya's encasement, the woman was gone. As he began falling to sleep, he heard Jericho's voice.

"You have five years. After that, we will release Mr. Green."

Wilson's eyelids became heavier as he stared at Jericho, trying to stay awake.

"I....know...." he responded.

"Beware of the beasts that come for you," Jericho's voice echoed.

Eventually, Wilson lost consciousness.

16

Two Weeks Later

"Wilson! Michael! Get up!"

Wilson rolled over and looked at the alarm clock. It was 6:30 in the morning. Suddenly the light went on, and his mother came into the room.

"Damn it, boys. We go through this every morning. Get your butts out of bed and hit the showers. Traffic will be hell on the GW Parkway on the first day of school. You're going to make your father late!"

Wilson raised his head to look at his mother. She was a blur as she moved through the room, picking up their clothes while putting on her earrings at the same time. She paused briefly and went to Michael's bed to slap him on the butt.

"Get up, Michael! Don't play with me!"

Wilson watched as his little brother rolled over and stared at him. Annoyed, their mother yanked the covers off of Michael.

"Get your ass out of bed! Now, Michael!

Michael stood up and yawned. After repositioning his junk in his underwear, he looked over at Wilson and smiled. Then he started complaining to his mother.

"Why do I always have to shower first? You never pressure Wilson the way you do me."

"You're the youngest, and you take the longest. The slowest showers first."

Wilson's mom walked quickly towards the door.

"When I come back, someone had better be dressed."

Michael walked towards the bathroom and paused to pass gas.

"I keep having the same dream last. I dreamed I was trapped inside a glass bottle."

Wilson looked at his little brother.

"Is that all you remember?"

"Yeah. Well, that plus Grandma Noya, she was inside a tree."

Michael walked into the bathroom and shut the door.

Wilson sat on the edge of his bed, staring at the bathroom door. Michael didn't remember anything about what happened, but he did. He remembered everything that Jericho told him and everything that would happen if he didn't comply. Wilson stood up and went to the mirror on his dresser. He noticed that his eye was just as it had been years ago; there was no discoloration or anything weird about his appearance.

"Son of a...."

Wilson reached up and touched his eyelid, and the whole room changed color just as before, revealing a world that no one could see but him. Quickly, he tapped his eyelid again, and the alternate world disappeared. Just as he did, Michael came out of the bathroom.

"Your turn, stink butt."

Wilson walked into the bathroom to shower and get ready for school.

17

Our Parents are Nuts

Wilson and Michael sat at the breakfast table watching their two parents fight.

"I don't like your friend."

Julia shrugged.

"I don't give a shit what you like, Dustin. Tammy is my friend, not yours."

Dustin frowned and slammed the newspaper on the table.

"There's so much we just don't know about her. Didn't you say her son got locked up for driving under the influence?"

Julia smirked at her husband.

"Don't do that. At least be a grown-up about your bullshit. You just don't like the fact that Tammy's Black."

"That's not true."

"Dustin, you're so full of shit. Stop with the self-hate for a minute. Your grandfather is Black, so what does that make you?"

"It makes me a concerned husband and father. I have a family to protect."

Julia bit into a piece of toast and grabbed her briefcase.

"I don't have time for this shit, Dustin. We can talk about it later."

Julia went around the table, kissing Wilson and then Michael.

"You boys have an awesome day at school. I want to hear all about it when you come home. Michael, remember to bring those books home. You can't study without books."

Michael sighed and shoved a spoonful of oatmeal into his mouth.

"Okay, mom."

Dustin held up his cheek. When Julia got to her husband, she ignored him and headed for the door.

"Bye, guys."

When she was gone, Wilson stared at his dad. Regardless of what was going on in the world, no amount of time would stop his parent's divorce.

Suddenly the front door opened again.

"Oh! I purchased some rat poison yesterday. It's underneath the sink. Don't put it down until after I get home. The boys and I will go and crash in a hotel overnight until it's finished."

Dustin frowned.

"Am I not welcome at the hotel?"

"Maybe in your own room. But with the boys and I, I doubt they'll be enough room. You know, with your gigantic ego and all."

Once again, Julia slammed the door. Michael got up and put his dishes in the sink.

"Our parents are crazy, Wilson," he said before heading to the bedroom.

Embarrassed, Dustin glanced at Wilson before standing up.

"Wilson, clear away the table. Tell Michael to get his things, and both of you meet me in the garage. I have a tight schedule today."

18

Old Friends

"Class, we have two new students today. You boys want to stand up?"

All the class turned around to look at the two new students.

"Say your names, please," instructed the teacher.

There was a scraping of chairs against the floor until two boys, an African American and a Native American, stood tall above the class.

"Tariq Johnson."

"Takatoka Kanoska."

Everything was quiet as the two boys squirmed in the unwanted attention. Suddenly a voice rang out.

"Now that's a mouthful!"

All the students broke into laughter – except one.

"Quiet down now. Does everyone have their class assignments?"

Everyone ignored the teacher and began talking amongst themselves.

"I know this is homeroom, guys, but you need to try to keep things down."

Wilson looked at Tariq and Takatoka. Without saying a word, they all gave the same emotionless stare to one another and quickly turned away.

****

"How much do you remember?" asked Takatoka.

"Almost everything except for the pain," replied Tariq while rubbing his legs.

"Well, that's good," said Wilson.

The three boys stopped at Wilson's locker and waited until a crowd of boys passed before continuing their conversation.

"So, what are you going to do?" asked Tariq.

Wilson shrugged.

"I'm not sure. I mean, how do you get millions of people out of the country? Do you guys have any ideas?"

"I do," whispered Tariq. "But none of them are good."

Wilson opened his locker and took out his lunch bag.

"You guys want to go get lunch?"

Both boys shook their heads in agreement.

"I feel weird," whispered Takatoka.

"What do you mean?" asked Wilson.

"Nobody knows what's going on—only us. It's like we're the adults, and everyone else is children. We have this huge responsibility, and we can't share it," explained Takatoka.

"Because if we did, they'd probably lock us up for being bat shit crazy," replied Tariq.

The boys continued walking until they came to the teachers' lounge.

"You guys go ahead. I'm going to ask Mrs. Penley for a referral to the counselor."

Tariq stared at Wilson.

"Problems at home?"

"It's weird. Jericho told me that nobody would remember a thing, but I'm not sure what my mom remembers. She seems more aggressive like she remembers all the problems in their relationship."

"A divorce?"

"In time, sure. But right now, I think mom's going to try to take Michael and me and run. I have to do something to stop her."

"It's cool, man. We'll go ahead and grab a table in the cafeteria."

As the two boys walked away from Wilson, he couldn't help feeling grateful for their presence. It was so much better to have friends in misery than none at all.

Wilson looked around to make sure no one was coming and entered the teachers' lounge.

A large tv sat in front of several long tables. Aside from the various food odors in the air, the room was empty. Sitting in the rear of the room was a large coffee maker. Someone had just started a new pot of coffee, and the coffee pot was filling up.

Wilson took a deep breath and unzipped his lunch bag. After listening to make sure no one was coming, he unzipped his lunch bag and pulled out a container of rat poison. Slowly, he went to the coffee pot and removed the carafe from the holder. Wilson shook in half of the poison, grabbed one of the nearby plastic spoons, and stirred the coffee. After the clumps of the powder dissolved, he put the carafe back onto the machine.

"For my family," Wilson whispered, trying his best to steady his nerves.

After checking the table next to the coffee pot to ensure he didn't leave anything behind, Wilson put the remaining rat poison back into his lunch bag. Slowly, he opened the door and looked around – the hallways were empty. He tucked his lunch bag under his arm and walked out of the teachers' lounge.

As soon as Wilson started walking, his hands began to shake, and he quickly shoved one of his hands into his jean pocket while the other clutched the rat poison. Soon his whole body began twitching as the weight of what he'd done fell on him like a ton of bricks - he was going to be a murderer, and as soon as some unsuspecting teacher drank the container of poison, his life would change forever.

Wilson stopped in the hallway. If he turned back now and went into the lounge to discard the coffee, no one would be the wiser to what he'd done. There would be no deaths, and Wilson could find another way to fulfill Jericho's sick demands.

Just as Wilson turned to go back to the teachers' lounge, he froze - a teacher, Mr. Behrend from Algebra, stood in front of the door fumbling with a stack of papers in one hand and an empty coffee cup in the other. Wilson was a statue of fear. He wanted to call out to the teacher.

Don't drink the coffee!

Those were the words Wilson wanted to say, but instead, all he could do was stand with his mouth open, unable to utter a single word. Finally, after struggling for a few moments, the teacher opened the door and went in. Utterly broken because he'd missed a chance to reverse his crime, Wilson's tears began pouring in earnest. Images of Mr. Behrend pouring himself a cup of coffee flooded his mind, making his knees wobble as he walked.

Before he turned the corner leading to the cafeteria, another teacher, Mrs. Harris, the Science teacher, arrived at the door of the teachers' lounge.

"Run!" Wilson whispered under his breath.

As if injected with a sudden burst of energy, Wilson broke into an all-out sprint towards the school exit. He had to get away before the bodies started falling.

www.ingramcontent.com/pod-product-compliance
Lightning Source LLC
Chambersburg PA
CBHW060419310726
48976CB00003B/1120